"Charles," she said, "unhand me, I beg of you."

"At last you have spoken my name," he whispered, drawing her closer, his hand gripping her waist. His lips touched hers tentatively at first and then with more certainty. The kiss was sweet and gentle, and although Jenna knew it was a scene he had enacted countless times with innumerable women, just then she felt it was the first and only time for both of them.

So engrossed were they in each other that neither heard approaching footsteps until a shocked voice broke into their heavenly idyll.

"Ye Gods! What a precious sight!"

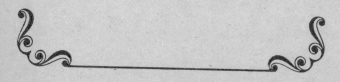

Fawcett Crest Books
by Rachelle Edwards:

FORTUNE'S CHILD

THE MARRIAGE BARGIN

DANGEROUS DANDY

AN UNEQUAL MATCH

REQENCY MASQUERADE

THE RANSOME
INHERITANCE

Rachelle Edwards

FAWCETT CREST • NEW YORK

A Fawcett Crest Book
Published by Ballantine Books
Copyright © 1983 by Rachelle Edwards
First published in Great Britian 1983

ISBN 0-449-21126-6

This edition published by arrangement with Robert Hale Limited

Manufactured in the United States of America

First Ballantine Books Edition: November 1986

ONE

The courtyard of *The Golden Fleece* resounded to the pounding hooves and of wheels rattling on cobbles. All at once the waiting ostlers stepped back smartly as the coach thundered into the courtyard and screeched to a halt. The horses were steaming, their nostrils flared, and the stage's paintwork was splattered liberally with a coating of mud and insects collected on the way, with the result that the original colour of the vehicle could not be guessed.

Almost as soon as the door was opened and the steps let down, passengers began to alight. Those who rode on top, prey to all the elements, could scarcely stand upright, and even those from the inside emerged pale and thankful to be safely at their destination.

As the ostlers hurried to and fro and the driver jumped from his perch crying, "Where's m'yard o'ale?" one of the inside passengers stepped down and paused by the coach to straighten her shabby pelisse and crumpled skirt. She was a slightly-built girl with wide blue eyes which bore a bewildered expression as she gazed around her.

There seemed to be a good deal of hurry-scurry in the yard. Not only had the West Country coach arrived, but the Mail was due to leave and there were several private chaises in the courtyard along with the people who were travelling in them. Bandboxes, cloakbags and trunks were piled everywhere, and the noise was deafening.

Jenna Tregail, who had just made the long and tedious journey from Penzance, found the number of people and the frenetic activity all around bewildering, and quite unexpected. Penzance had been the busiest place she had known up until then, but this bore no comparison to that little backwater.

After a few moments she stepped forward and asked timidly of an ostler, "May I leave my box here for a while?"

"It's not the likes of me you're wantin' to ask, Miss. You'd best ask of the landlord."

"Where may I . . . ?"

Before she could finish her question he had hurried away to heave up a box against his leather apron. Jenna looked about her, feeling all the more bewildered. Another lackey placed a box at her feet.

"This yours, Miss?"

Jenna started. "Oh yes, but . . ."

Too late. He had gone to unload more of the luggage. The horses had been uncoupled and were being led away to a well-earned rest. Jenna stepped back sharply as they were led past her.

She turned away in dismay to seek out the landlord of the inn. Suddenly she swayed slightly on her feet. She put one hand up to her head and realised what ailed her was hunger, for she had not eaten for hours. She could scarcely recall her last good meal. The fare served up to the coach passengers at the inns along the way had been most unappetising, and the constant jolting of the vehicle had not made hearty eating advisable, although Jenna had noted that several of her fellow passengers did indulge in a substantial meal at every stop.

As she approached the inn door three young bucks came out, almost knocking her off her feet. Jenna gasped, they laughed but did not trouble to steady her or to apologise. They hurried away, still laughing as Jenna stared after them. Then she stood up and straightened her bonnet out of which peeped a mass of undisciplined curls, the colour of ripe corn.

"Got no manners, some of these Corinthians," a voice behind her commented.

Jenna turned on her heel to see a woman, elegantly clad in a velvet pelisse and feathered bonnet. Her face was creased with concern and Jenna warmed to her immediately. After all, this was the first friendly voice she had heard and Jenna's face broke into a smile.

"I dare say I shall have to grow accustomed to such behaviour now I am in London."

The woman, who was well past her youth but handsome for all that, looked interested. "Just arrived, have you? On the West Country Flyer?"

Jenna lowered her lashes. "It must be obvious I am a stranger and totally bewildered."

"Where are you bound? London is a big city."

Jenna smiled again. "So I am discovering, ma'am. I'm not settled, as yet, and I was hoping to be able to leave my box here for a while until I can send for it."

The woman's eyes narrowed. "Haven't you got anywhere to go?"

"No, not yet, I fear."

The woman looked dismayed. "That is not wise, my dear. There are pitfalls for young ladies alone." Jenna stared at her uncomprehendingly and the other woman cast her a smile. "Never you fear. I shall set you right." She put her head on one side. "I was just about to go inside and order some breakfast. Will you join me?"

Jenna's face grew pink. "I wouldn't wish to . . ."

3

The woman brushed past her, going inside. "Come along, child. I am famished and I'll warrant you are too."

Jenna could not argue on that score. The thought of a meal now was most welcome. The landlord was coming towards them and his face broke into a knowing smile.

"Why, Mrs Creevy, how may I be of service to you today?" He glanced at Jenna too and she fancied there was a look of pity there also, which puzzled her.

"A private parlour for me and my friend, Mr Perrit, and breakfast, if you please. Oh, and pray take care of this young lady's box until she is ready for it."

"Certainly. You need have no qualms, Miss. It will be taken care of. This way, if you please, ladies."

He ushered them into a private parlour where a welcoming fire burned brightly in the hearth. Mrs Creevy removed her bonnet and patted her dark hair into place. Jenna did likewise and when she had removed her mittens she went immediately to the fire to warm her hands.

Watching her Mrs Creevy observed, "You must be frozen after that journey. Coaches are such draughty conveyances."

Jenna smiled. "Yes, indeed. I was for ever rubbing my hands to keep them warm."

"Travelling is no pleasure, is it, my dear?" Mrs Creevy asked.

Jenna chuckled. "It is a dreadful experience. Apart from the cold, I was quite persuaded the coachman was bosky most of the time, and at one stage a young man tipped him a guinea to take the ribbons. It was terrifying. I thought we should all be killed."

"I often wonder why people travel at all, unless it is of dire necessity. Apart from the cold and the terrible discomfort, one is fortunate not to encounter a tobyman. Only necessity would induce me to travel any distance. Kensington is far enough for me."

4

She cast Jenna a speculative look as the girl turned around. Some vestige of colour had returned to her cheeks. Jenna thought the way Mrs Creevy was considering her was rather odd, but a moment later the woman asked, "What is your name, my dear? I don't believe you made mention of it."

"I do beg your pardon, ma'am. My name is Jenna Tregail. It is very good of you to invite me for breakfast."

"You mustn't mention it. I like company and you did appear to be a trifle bewildered."

"I was indeed. I have never seen so much activity or so many people in one place."

Mrs Creevy smiled. "London is a bewildering place for those unused to the pace. A dangerous place too."

It was then that breakfast arrived, brought in by two maidservants who eyed Jenna with interest as they set the table. When they had gone both ladies sat down at the table and ate their fill from the ample selection of dishes.

"Have you also just arrived in London?" Jenna enquired as she buttered just another slice of bread.

"No. . . . As I said, I loathe travel. I had just seen a friend onto the Mail." Mrs Creevy put down her cup. "What brings you to London, my dear? Are you visiting relatives perchance?"

"No," Jenna answered with some difficulty. "I know no one in London as yet."

Mrs Creevy sat back in her chair and stared wide-eyed at the younger woman. "Truly? Why on earth are you here?"

"To seek employment. I hope to become a governess or a companion in some respectable family. I believe I am well qualified, having been companion to my aunt for several years."

"Indeed, that may well be so, but you are also a trifle too fetching, I declare. There are those who might deem it a disadvantage." Jenna's cheeks grew pink and the woman went on, "Such positions are not easy to obtain, even for those well qualified. You do have a letter of recommendation with you?"

Jenna was taken aback. "Oh, no. I . . ."

"Why did you not find a situation nearer your home?" Jenna stared into the fire, her face a picture of misery. "You do not have to tell me. It was impertinent of me to ask."

"No, no," Jenna protested. "I don't mind. You have been so kind and you are sympathetic."

"I am honoured you think so my dear," Mrs Creevy told her, smiling sweetly. "It might well ease your burden if you do confide in me. I am often told I have a sympathetic countenance."

"After my parents died I lived with my aunt for several years. She was never a well woman but when she knew she had little time left to live she charged my cousin, her daughter, to care for me after she was gone. Letty did so for a while. She was a widow and I lived with her although in truth she and I were sadly dissimilar, but then she became betrothed and naturally wished . . ."

"Not to have such a pretty distraction for her new husband," Mrs Creevy supplied, and Jenna's cheeks grew pink again. "Oh, 'tis understandable. I have seen such situations before."

Jenna drew herself up straight. "I shall contrive, you may be sure."

"Indeed you will. You possess a true spirit which I admire and others will do so too. Even so, my dear, you have never been obliged to fend for yourself in what is truly a cruel world."

Jenna got to her feet, feeling distinctly reluctant to venture once more into the uncaring world outside. Nevertheless she said, "I really must go now." She began to

6

fumble in her reticule and brought out some coins. "This, I believe, will cover the cost of the food."

Mrs Creevy also stood up. "Do not trouble. I intended to buy breakfast for myself and I have enjoyed our conversation and your company."

Returning the coins to the reticule Jenna smiled gratefully. "You have been very kind," she said as she put on her bonnet. "I am obliged to you, ma'am, but I must make haste now if I am to find accommodation."

As Jenna moved towards the door Mrs Creevy said thoughtfully, "Don't go so quickly. A notion has just come to me." As Jenna looked at her curiously she went on, "A friend of mine is sadly an invalid. Her husband, only a sen'night ago, mentioned the desire to engage a companion for her. . . ."

Jenna began to look hopeful, hardly daring to believe her good fortune. She had begun to wonder if she would after all, find employment in London. Nothing was as she had imagined it to be.

"Oh, that would be wonderful!" she gasped. "Do you truly believe . . . ? I have had experience with invalids. Aunt Zillah . . ."

Mrs Creevy laughed and held up her hand. "We shall see. You must not be too hopeful and I cannot promise anything." She picked up her bonnet and began to walk towards Jenna who was near the door. "It would be best if you came home with me and whilst you wash and rest I shall send a note to my friend's house."

Jenna clasped her hands together. "I could not impose upon you further, Mrs Creevy."

"I insist upon it. 'Tis no trouble, I assure you."

"How shall I ever thank you?"

"What tush. I consider it a favour to my friend. The longer I ponder upon it, the more I am persuaded you are exactly suited to the post he has in mind."

7

Jenna walked out into the courtyard, feeling much happier than when she had entered. The Mail and the stage-coach had left, and only a few private carriages remained. Mrs Creevy paused to pay for the breakfast, enabling Jenna to conserve her small funds. A few moments later her prospective benefactor came out of the inn, smoothing on her gloves.

"The landlord assures me he will look after your box until you are settled. If we walk to the corner we shall be able to hail a hackney."

"Do you live far from here?" Jenna asked.

"A little way, but too far to walk. My house is close by Covent Garden Market which is a convenient location."

"It must be near to the famous Opera House."

"That too."

A young gooseherd was ushering his flock along the footpath, causing both ladies to pause until he and his geese had passed.

"I should like so much to go there," Jenna murmured longingly.

"I do have my own box at the Opera House," Mrs Creevy confided as they paused yet again to avoid the swinging pails of a milkmaid who was passing. "I allow those to whom I am very partial to use it."

At such a revelation Jenna could only stare at her in awe as she waved to a hackney which was passing at the far side of the street.

"Your own box! How wonderful that must be to be able to attend whenever you wish."

"And so may you, my dear, as my own guest."

"Oh, Mrs Creevy, I am quite speechless."

"You might even be fortunate enough to see the Prince of Wales there one evening. He attends often, as do most of the *haute ton*."

"I cannot imagine being in such elevated company."

8

A high-perch phaeton came bowling around the corner, driven by an elegant young buck. Jenna had been about to cross the road when the other woman pulled her back and she missed being knocked down by a hair's breadth. The phaeton passed on, unaware of the near catastrophe, but several passers-by stopped to stare, much to Jenna's embarrassment.

"You will be obliged to take heed when crossing the streets," Mrs Creevy warned her.

"Indeed I shall," the girl agreed, still breathless.

The number of carriages on the streets amazed Jenna, not to mention the number of people who crowded along the footpaths. She had never seen so much activity, even in Penzance. The hackney was waiting when they did manage to cross the street and both ladies climbed in. It was fairly clean inside with fresh straw on the floor. However, Jenna was more interested in what was outside the carriage to notice such things.

As the hackney made its way towards Covent Garden, Jenna thought that some of the buildings looked a trifle ramshackle and a good many people appeared to be desperately poor, but no more so than many of the farm labourers she had seen in Cornwall. The problem was, she had been led to believe no one living in London was in want. On the contrary, it was rumoured that everyone who came to London soon became very rich.

By way of contrast, though, Jenna also noticed many elegantly dressed people, mainly those travelling in carriages, who wore some of the finest clothes she had ever seen. Even looking from the window of the carriage, the countless shops seemed to be displaying a dazzling array of merchandise, reinforcing her belief that most inhabitants of the city were indeed wealthy. Even the modest-looking Mrs Creevy had her own box at the Opera House.

Mrs Creevy smiled gently, seemingly aware of some of

Jenna's thoughts. "When you have an income of your own you will be able to do more than gaze at the shops. Some of the merchandise is quite dazzling. Silks from China, cotton from the Indies."

"I scarce dare think it will be possible."

"It is entirely possible for a female to earn a great deal of money in this city."

"I should be glad of a modest payment, I assure you, ma'am. The money I have by me will not last for ever."

Mrs Creevy patted her hand reassuringly. "You have no need to fret. My . . . friend will welcome you on my recommendation."

The carriage pulled up in front of a handsome house with a row of neat railings outside. Jenna gazed at it admiringly as Mrs Creevy paid the jarvey.

"Is Mr Creevy at home?" Jenna asked, wondering belatedly if he might object to a stranger being brought into his house.

"Alas I am a widow," the woman replied as a liveried footman opened the door to them.

Jenna stepped into a lofty hall lit by a large crystal chandelier. Several rooms led off the hall and some had their doors open to reveal luxurious furnishings. Jenna was once again surprised, for Mrs Creevy had not appeared so wealthy, although Jenna admitted to being no judge of such matters.

Mrs Creevy stripped off her gloves and handed them to the lackey. "Have any messages been left for me?"

"Lord Meekin, ma'am. He intends to call tonight and asks that Violet . . ."

"Yes, yes," the woman answered hastily, "you had better tell me later. Ah, Cooper, show Miss Tregail to a guest room. She has just arrived on the stage and is exceeding weary."

An elderly maidservant hurried up to them and Mrs

Creevy went on, addressing Jenna, "Try to rest, my dear. I shall go immediately to pen the note, and I am persuaded we shall very quickly receive an answer."

"This way, Miss," Cooper instructed, moving towards the curving staircase.

Mrs Creevy hurried into one of the rooms and Jenna transferred her attention to the maid who was looking at her with rather an insolent expression. Jenna followed her up the stairs, amazed at the luxury and opulence all around her. Gilt cupids adorned several niches lining the staircase and some of the statues in others obliged her to avert her eyes. When they reached the wide landing a door opened ever so slightly. Curious, Jenna looked around in time to see a pair of startled eyes staring out at her. Jenna smiled faintly but a moment later the door closed as quietly as it had opened.

Farther along the corridor Cooper flung open a door and waited patiently for Jenna to precede her into the room which was very well appointed, with a half-tester bed, large press and dressing table. The furniture was very handsome, matching the opulence Jenna had glimpsed elsewhere in the house. Several Turkey rugs tempered the bare floor and murky prints hung on the walls.

Jenna immediately went ot the window and found she had a fine view of the Piazza and some of its vendors. A tingle of excitement went down her spine and she felt that life, from now on, must surely be better than it had been of late. A feeling of sadness pervaded her whenever she reflected that all those she loved were dead, and there was no one in the entire world who cared if she lived or died, except perhaps for Mrs Creevy. Cousin Letty had only been too delighted that she was leaving, although Jenna had detected signs of regret in Mr FitzGibbon.

"May I take your bonnet and pelisse, Miss?" the maid asked.

Jenna turned on her heel and smiled at the woman. "Thank you."

When Cooper had carefully put Jenna's shabby clothes into the press, the maid said, "The girl will be up with hot water soon, but if there's anything else you require just ring."

No sooner had Cooper gone than a maid, no more than a girl, arrived with a jug of hot water. She glanced at Jenna curiously as she put it down on the marble wash-stand and giggled before hurrying out again.

Jenna realised then that she was indeed weary. Sleeping on a jolting coach, crushed close to others, was impossible. The inns at which they had put up at night were not of the best. The beds were far from clean, the sheets not properly aired, and noises from the inns and courtyards seemed to go on all night. Jenna glanced at the bed with longing and as soon as the maid had gone she took off her gown and washed in the fragrant water before climbing between the fresh sheets. The bed felt as soft as it had looked and she sank into it, revelling in the luxury.

Sleep did not claim her at once, however. Lots of images went through her mind; her departure from Penzance when Cousin Letty did not even wait long enough to see her on the coach, her bewildering arrival, the meeting with Mrs Creevy, and this large house. Jenna could not help but wonder who else might live there, for she heard frequent footsteps in the corridor. At one point she could hear someone talking in low, urgent tones outside the door, and somewhere not too far away high-pitched laughter. However, before long exhaustion overcame her and Jenna slept deeply and dreamlessly at last.

TWO

Elegant was the only way to describe Branston Manor, a small Queen Anne house nestling amidst rolling lawns and shady arbours just outside the village of Burnham Padgett in the county of Kent.

Members of the Ransome family had lived in the area for centuries, and successive generations had added to the oringinal dwelling house, improving as their fortunes increased. The Ransome fortune was based in the Indies, trade in silks, tea and latterly slaves from Africa—something which was never mentioned—had made them immensely wealthy, and anyone who rode up the long, curving driveway could ascertain that fact at a glance.

On this particular day, when the poplars which lined the driveway were leafless and a cold wind whipped through the branches, a small procession of carriages came slowly through the gates. The hooves of every horse was muffled and each wore black ribbons. When the first carriage came to a halt outside the porticoed entrance to the house, three people, all dressed in deepest black, climbed down.

First was a slightly-built young man whose mourning outfit could not disguise that he was something of a dandy. He paused to hand down a lady whose black veil fluttered in the wind. The third person to climb down was an elderly gentleman whose frizzed wig proclaimed him a lawyer.

"What a sad business," he murmured as he climbed down. "And so shockingly sudden despite Mr Ransome's ill-health."

"My brother was not an old man," the woman replied, "but his spirit was broken a long time ago. At least we can hope he is now at peace."

"Amen to that," the lawyer responded.

The woman glanced up at the house's facade as the other carriages continued to the servants' entrance at the side of the building. "To think that this house was once filled with Ransomes. It is hard to believe so few of us are left. What will become of it now?"

The young man touched her arm. "Do not distress yourself, Mama. Uncle Jack would not have wished it."

She smiled at him fondly and took his arm as they walked up the wide flight of steps. When they reached the spacious hall, dominated by the twin staircases and marble statuary brought back from Italy by the young John Ransome, the woman threw back her veil and began to remove her gloves.

"My brother separated himself from his neighbours so successfully scarce a handful attended the service."

"It was the way he wished to live, Mama."

"Mr Fordyce is correct, ma'am," the lawyer agreed, "and now, with your permission I shall see everyone is assembled in the library."

Harriet Fordyce was once a great beauty but now only remnants of her glory remained. She sucked in a sharp breath. "Naturally, Mr Prichett. Pray do so. Gerald and I will join you presently, but I must have a few moments to compose myself."

As he hurried away she turned to her son. "I shall be glad when this business is over."

Gerald Fordyce adjusted his perfectly folded neckcloth before flicking open his diamond-studded snuff box. "Don't be in such a fidge, Mama. There is no one else to whom Uncle Jack could have left his fortune. I was, after all, his favourite nephew."

"But not his only one." She twisted her hands together in anguish. "My brother was never predictable, Gerald. Abigail was always his favourite sister, not I."

"She is dead." He took a pinch of snuff and returned the box to his pocket, flicking the flecks which remained off the sleeve of his coat.

"Her son is not. You must not forget there is another nephew with as much claim as you."

Gerald Fordyce smiled. "Hollingdale is a scapegrace, Mama. Moreover he has scarce set eyes upon Uncle Jack in years. It is not something like to endear him to our uncle who enjoyed my dancing attendance upon him. 'Tis so unlike you to fret."

"Indeed." She drew in a deep breath. "It is merely that I am concerned for you, Gerald. This house, the fortune, is yours by right, and I am anxious to have the matter settled."

"And so it will be—very soon."

The house-steward was approaching. "Mr Pritchett requests your presence in the library."

Once again Harriet Fordyce took her son's arm. "It was the death of his wife and child so close together which seemed to unhinge his reason a little. Before that he was as normal as you or I."

"That was all a long time ago, Mama."

"First the one and then the other. He never recovered fully. Poor, poor Jack. I was once very fond of him."

The servants were assembled in the library and Harriet Fordyce and her son took their places at the front of the gathering. One chair nearby was vacant, that allocated to

Charles Hollingdale, the only other member of the family still living. The empty chair stressed his absence more forcibly than anything else could do.

The lawyer cleared his throat and began to read the last will and testament of John Cedric Ransome. There was, as expected, a lengthy list of minor bequests. Most of the servants had been at the Manor for a very long time, and the terms of the will reflected their late master's recognition of this.

"To my housekeeper, Mrs Mary Tarrand, I bequeath the sum of one hundred guineas in recognition . . ."

The housekeeper gasped and then began to sob quietly into her handkerchief. Gerald Fordyce was tapping gently on the arm of his chair, the only outward revelation of his inner concern. His mother glanced at him, smiling faintly. Soon they would know.

The lawyer put down the document. "That concludes the minor bequests. If the rest of you would care to go about your duties now . . ."

Chairs scraped back on the wooden floor and a low murmuring accompanied the servants' departure from the library. Gerald Fordyce was now clutching the arms of his chair and his knuckles were white. When the last of the servants, all still clad in their sombre Sunday attire, left the room, the lawyer began to intone once more.

"To my sister, Harriet Maude Fordyce, I bequeath my late wife's emerald ring and her pearl necklet together with a sum of one thousand guineas."

Harriet Fordyce began to sniff into her lace-edged handkerchief whilst her son shifted uneasily in his seat. The lawyer put down the parchment and looked at them.

"Mr Ransome had a strong sense of family obligation," he began. Gerald Fordyce smiled faintly as his mother dabbed at her eyes. "I think, in the circumstances I had best explain Mr Ransome's wishes for the remainder of his estate."

Mr Pritchett folded his hands together on the top of the desk and Gerald eased his collar a little. "You may not have been aware of this, but Mr Ransome remained convinced that his daughter, Annabel, was still alive . . ."

Gerald sat up straight in the chair and his mother gasped, "That's absurd!"

"Be that as it may, Mrs Fordyce, Mr Ransome has charged me as lawyer and executor to attempt to trace his missing daughter." Again there was a gasp. "The terms of the will are these: an exhaustive search must be undertaken to find Miss Annabel Ransome, and it is she who is presently heir to the fortune."

"She is dead!" Gerald cried. "Searchers have been made in the past to no avail!"

"Nevertheless, Mr Ransome's wishes in the matter are very clear. The search, undertaken by me and my colleagues, is to last not longer than five years."

"And then . . . ?" Harriet Fordyce asked anxiously.

"After which time if the missing heiress in not found or indeed proved to be dead, the Ransome estates and monies are to be divided equally between you, Mr Fordyce, and your cousin Major . . ." he consulted the will, "Charles Devlin Ransome Hollingdale."

Gerald's eyes almost stood out of his head and his mother jumped to her feet, her face pale her eyes dark with anger. "Mr Pritchett, you must see that this is absurd."

"I did attempt to argue Mr Ransome out of it, but he insisted. There was nothing more I could do."

"The child is dead," Gerald said in bewilderment. "It was always considered so. Uncle Jack acknowledged the fact years ago. There is a plaque in her name in Burnham Padgett church!"

Mr Pritchett smiled faintly. "I do commiserate with you, sir, but there never was any proof of death."

"She was playing by the river when she disappeared. What more proof is required?"

"No body was ever found. It was Mr Ransome's belief his daughter was abducted by gypsies who were in the area. The question did arise at the time of the disappearance but they were never traced, you may recall."

"It it is so, they never will be now," Harriet Fordyce said harshly.

The lawyer began to gather up his documents. "I am entirely in agreement with you, madam, but I am obliged to abide by the terms of my client's will. A search will be started immediately and I shall keep you apprised of the progress. If I can be of any further service to you both in the meantime you know where I can be contacted. And now, pray excuse me; I must return to London now if I am to reach it by dark. Your servant, ma'am, sir."

He backed out of the room and the moment he had gone Gerald let out a gasp of exasperation. "I can scarce credit this."

"I feared something of this nature," his mother cried. "The old fool."

"What can have made him think she might still be alive? Annabel will never be found," his mother said then with certainly. "How can she be? If she is alive, which all of us doubt, she will be all of one and twenty, and a true gypsy. No, 'tis impossible."

Her son strode across to the window to watch the lawyer's departure. "Even so I shall be obliged to wait for five years and then . . ." his face twisted into a grimace, "to share with Hollingdale. Oh, Mama, 'tis so unjust."

Harriet Fordyce walked to and fro, wringing her hands. "That scapegrace. He has not shown his face here for the

18

past five years at least. It is useless to say my brother's mind was unhinged when he made the will, for I always suspected it."

As the lawyer's carriage rumbled away Gerald came back from the window. "Hollingdale's absence might have something to do with being with his regiment which is fighting Boney."

She sat down again, cradling her head in one hand. "Tush. Don't seek to protect him."

"As if I would."

"He was always too busy, even before he joined the army; gambling, light-skirts, duelling. It isn't just, Gerald. You have been so devoted to Jack, and now to be repaid in this fashion. . . ."

The young man drew in a deep sigh. "Indeed, Mama, but I cannot perceive what we can do about it. Just now I would as lief share the estate with Hollingdale as be in this situation. My pockets are to let, I must own, and I'm in a devil of a fix."

Harriet Fordyce laughed harshly. 'When are you not in dun territory?" She moaned softly then. "Pour me a measure of brandy. My head aches abominably."

"Ah, brandy! That is an excellent suggestion, Mama. Uncle Jack possessed only the finest French brandy. Boney never put an end to that supply."

He went to where decanters and glasses were set out upon a silver tray on a drum table, and poured two generous measures of the amber liquid. He took one to his mother and after a few moments sat down on the edge of the desk, staring down at his highly-polished Hessian boots before he raised his glass, smiling ironically.

"To Uncle Jack, wherever he may be."

"I cannot find it in my heart to echo that toast, Gerald. The fortune should have been yours and now."

He savoured a mouthful of brandy. "One can only hope no trace of the chit can be found. Even so . . ." he added with a sigh.

Harriet Fordyce put down her empty glass. "Gerald, what if she is found? And quickly?"

He shrugged. "It is the worst thing that can happen. In that event I shall not even inherit *half*."

"You misunderstand me." Harriet Fordyce's eyes were wide with excitement. "I don't mean the real Annabel. She was, as like or not, drowned in the river and swept out to sea. What I meant was an Annabel chosen by us to claim the inheritance."

He put down his glass on the desk. "I'm beginning to see what you mean, Mama." For a moment he was thoughtful and then he shook his head. "It couldn't possibly work."

"Do not be so certain."

"What female would want to undertake such a pretence, bearing in mind we cannot employ anyone even remotely connected with us."

"I am aware of that. It must be someone who has no choice but to do our bidding."

"And where would you find anyone like that, Mama?"

"I have a notion," she answered thouoghtfully. She waved her hand in the air. "We shall return to London and think on it—very carefully."

Gerald smiled as he quaffed the last dregs of brandy and then got to his feet. "Oh, indeed we shall, Mama."

THREE

For several moments after she woke up Jenna could not recall where she was. At first she thought she was still in her room in Cousin Letty's cottage, but that was only a quarter of the size of this one, and had a sloping roof. From somewhere within the house there came the sound of activity and voices, some of them rather loud although she could not make out what they were actually saying.

With a start Jenna sat up, recalling where she was at last. Dusk had fallen and the room was almost in darkness. The fire had died down and she felt cold, clad only in her shift. Outside, not too far away, the watch was calling the hour and there seemed to be a continual clatter of carriage wheels on the cobbled street outside.

The door began to open slowly to admit a long shaft of light. Jenna pulled the covers up further, peering anxiously through the gloom towards the door. A girl, holding a candle, entered slowly, looking fearful; then she hesitated before closing the door quietly behind her.

"Who . . . who are you?" Jenna asked, aware that the girl was not dressed as a maidservant.

"Anne. My name's Anne."

Jenna thought this might well be the same person who

21

had peered at her when she arrived. Anne put the candle down on the table which lent a little light to the room, but left the corners still in shadow.

"Are you Mrs Creevy's daughter?" Jenna asked, for this seemed to be the logical explanation.

"No," the girl replied in a harsh whisper. "I am no relation to that woman."

"Do you live here?"

"Yes." The word was almost a sob.

She seemed ill at ease, but when she came closer to the bed Jenna noted that she was wearing a beautiful satin gown although its neckline was not at all modest.

Jenna looked away as Anne demanded, "Why are you here?"

Taken aback by the girl's hostile attitude, Jenna stammered, "I am . . . here only until I find a suitable position."

The girl leaned closer and asked in a low voice, "Where did you encounter Mrs Creevy?"

"At the Golden Fleece. I arrived on the West Country stage. Mrs Creevy very kindly took pity upon me."

"Pity," the girl scoffed.

Jenna gazed at her again, curious about her odd mood. The girl clenched her hands convulsively in front of her.

"If you have any wits about you, you will leave here now. Go quickly and do not hesitate."

Jenna laughed in bewilderment. "I intend to as soon as Mrs Creevy has obtained the post for me, or at least an interview."

The door opened again and Mrs Creevy herself stood framed in the doorway in a halo of light. She was holding a candle and became very angry when she saw Anne. Just for a second the look on Mrs Creevy's face made Jenna shiver. Anne started nervously and hurried away from the bed.

"Anne," the woman said sharply, "why are you here? Why do you disturb Miss Tregail?"

Mrs Creevy came further into the room as Anne replied, "I thought I heard Miss Tregail cry out."

Mrs Creevy eyed the girl coldly. "You'd best go downstairs. Our guests are arriving and you should be there to greet them."

The girl hurried to do her bidding, pausing only momentarily to glance back at Jenna. Mrs Creevy watched her go and then closed the door, shutting out some of the noise drifting up from downstairs.

Her demeanour immediately softened. "I'm so sorry about that, my dear. I do hope she did not . . . disturb you."

"No, indeed. I was already awake when she arrived, but she did seem a trifle overset."

The older woman sighed. "She is a trial to me, I own."

"And yet she lives here, does she not?"

Mrs Creevy looked upset. "She has nowhere else to go. She is not so well endowed as you, and I cannot find her suitable employment. I . . . helped her escape an unfortunate life and allow her to live here with me, but she rarely exhibits any gratitude and is often a trial to me."

Jenna slipped her feet over the side of the bed, noting that her hostess was dressed in a rose-coloured velvet gown of a modish design with feathers in her hair.

"What a buffle-head she must be. I cannot credit such ingratitude."

The woman's eyes narrowed and, shading the flame, she put down the candle. "What . . . did she say to you? Nothing untoward, I trust."

Jenna smiled. "She was merely urging me to leave here."

"How shabby of her!"

23

Jenna smiled reassuringly. "It was only envy, I should think."

"Yes, indeed, but Anne is not your problem, my dear, and I do have good news to impart. My friend is very anxious to make your acquaintance and requests your presence this very evening! My carriage will take you there with no further delay."

Jenna could hardly believe her good fortune. "Oh, Mrs Creevy, that is indeed splendid news! I had not hoped to hear so soon."

The door opened yet again to admit, this time, Cooper who had some clothing over her arm. "I thought," Mrs Creevy told Jenna, "you would make a better impression upon Mr Quint—for that is my friend's name—if you wore a more modish gown. This, I believe, will fit you admirably."

Mrs Creevy took the gown from Cooper and held it up for Jenna's inspection. Jenna was astonished. The gown was beautiful, but quite unlike anything she had ever worn before. High-waisted and low-necked in white chiffon, the hem was covered in thousands of tiny silver beads.

Jenna gasped. "It's beautiful and I do thank you, but surely not suited . . ."

"Allow me to know what is best, my dear. After all, London is not Penzance and a trifle more sophistication is required."

The admonishment caused Jenna to blush and Mrs Creevy went on as if unaware of it, "Try it on and let us judge then." When Jenna still hesitated the woman urged, "Do put it on if only to please me."

This last plea caused Jenna to hesitate no longer, but she still felt rather foolish. However, the sight of herself in the gown almost made her gasp, for the transformation was amazing. The glamorous creature who stared back from the mirror was almost a stranger.

24

"See," Mrs Creevy cooed, "you look quite beautiful. I knew you would. You must allow me to guide you in such matters."

"I still cannot help but think it is far too good," Jenna protested as Cooper remade the fire and lit more candles.

The maid drew the heavy velvet curtains across the window, shutting out the sounds of the London night. Although her own reflection pleased her, Jenna was still privately doubtful about its suitability, but bowed to what she believed must be Mrs Creevy's superior knowledge in the matter.

She allowed Cooper to arrange her curls into an elegant style to which she was also quite unused.

"I should really be attending a rout," Jenna joked when she got up from the dressing-table, feeling self-conscious about her new appearance. The most surprising part was the ease with which the transformation had been made.

"And so you shall," Mrs Creevy promised, "when you return from Mr Quint's. I have a great many guests downstairs, and I'm persuaded they will wish to make your acquaintance."

"I am keeping you from your guests," Jenna apologised. "How thoughtless of me. I am so sorry."

Mrs Creevy placed a cloak about Jenna's shoulders. "They won't miss me for a while. The carriage is waiting for you downstairs. Don't disappoint Mr Quint or me."

Jenna cast her a look filled with gratitude. "How could I after all your kindness to me?"

"There is just one thing," the older woman cautioned, and then smiled. "Mr Quint has long been concerned for his wife's well-being. There are things about him which you might find a trifle odd at first, but I beg of you be indulgent."

Cooper busied herself tidying the room as Jenna followed

25

Mrs Creevy towards the door. "What kind of things?" she asked.

Mrs Creevy laughed. "Well, it is like you will notice nothing amiss."

The woman hurried out into the corridor and Jenna had little option but to follow. She felt both nervous and happy; a congenial post was all she hoped for and it seemed she would have one very soon.

The noise from downstairs was louder now. A drunken buck ran past them, chasing a girl who was wearing a flimsy chiffon gown. Mrs Creevy smiled encouragingly at Jenna who paused to watch the chase in astonishment.

"A hostess is obliged to provide wine for her guests, but there are those who do not know when to stop drinking it. However, you may be quite certain that is one young man who will not receive an invitation in future. His behaviour is outside of enough."

As they passed the room which Jenna believed belonged to Anne, the young maidservant was just coming out. She glanced meaningfully at Mrs Creevy and Jenna thought she heard the sound of weeping briefly before the door was closed. Mrs Creevy, however, seemed not to notice.

Jenna followed her down the stairs. There appeared to be a great many people in the house. Oddly most of them were men. The empty rooms Jenna had glimpsed earlier were now crowded with people. As she came slowly down the stairs she could see that many of them were gambling or behaving in an immodest manner with the women present. Some of the men turned to stare at her, which caused Jenna's cheeks to redden. She was glad to reach the carriage, for she did not much like Mrs Creevy's guests and hoped, when she returned, she would not be obliged to join them.

As the carriage moved away Jenna found herself surprised at the way in which she had seen her hostess's guests conduct themselves. Ladies had been in what could only be described as dishabille, and the men appeared to be more than a little bosky. Of course, she had heard that society routs were often wild affairs. However she did hope that the Quints did not hold such diversions. If Mrs Quint was a chronic invalid it was unlikely that they did, and the thought pleased her. A quiet congenial post was all she sought.

At night the streets of London were no less crowded than during the day. The lights everywhere were dazzling. A number of very elegant carriages, all with escutcheons emblazoned upon their doors, were on their way to the Opera House. Some, however, stopped outside Mrs Creevy's house, but once they were away from the immediate area of Covent Garden, the carriage bowled along towards Oxford Street with its shops, more dazzling than those Jenna had seen earlier in the day. It seemed incredible that only a few days earlier she had faced the fact that living with Cousin Letty would no longer be possible. Until then she had not thought of leaving. She had often caught sight of John FitzGibbon eyeing her in a way she had come to recognise in men. It was the day Mr FitzGibbon slipped his arm around her waist that she realised she would have to move on. Cousin Letty had not demurred, indicating that she too was aware of the problem, and had even provided enough money to see Jenna on her way. She felt momentarily sad at the demise of her old and familiar way of life, but she experienced a certain excitement too, for an entirely new one was about to begin.

The carriage moved slowly into a tree-shaded square. The houses evidently belonged to those with sufficient wealth to maintain them handsomely and Jenna was immediately impressed.

"Here we are, Miss," the driver told her. "Number eleven is where you want to be."

27

The tiger handed her down and as she was about to approach the front door at either side of which burned two lamps, the lackey whispered, "The servants' entrance, Miss."

Jenna swallowed convulsively and was glad that the dark hid her reddening cheeks. "Oh, of course."

The tiger cast her a cheeky grin as she moved away. However, the door was opened almost as soon as she arrived there. A liveried servant holding up a branch of candles led her through dark corridors and up the back stairs. It occurred to Jenna that this was an odd way to approach such an interview, but supposed the sooner it was done, the earlier she would be settled. At that moment Jenna decided she would buy Mrs Creevy a gift in appreciation of her concern. It was the least she could do.

The house seemed to be a large one, even more spacious than Mrs Creevy's, but that might well have been because there were few people about, unlike the other house.

At last it seemed she had arrived when the lackey flung open the door to a small drawing-room. Jenna felt apprehensive, afraid she would not after all please her prospective employer. Being companion to Aunt Zillah who loved her, was not quite the same as living with strangers.

"Come in, come in do, my dear," a voice urged, the moment the door was opened.

The room, like the rest of the house, was dimly lit, only two branches of candles and no wall sconces. A small, rotund man of middle age came hurrying to greet her. He wore a brocade dressing-gown and a tasselled cap.

As soon as Jenna entered the room, the man dismissed the lackey, saying, "That will be all, Dooley," and then he returned his attention to her. "Allow me to take your cloak, my dear."

Although she felt nervous she allowed him to do so and he placed it carefully over the back of a sofa.

"Mrs Creevy speaks highly of you," he told her, eyeing her carefully. He seemed pleased with what he saw but for some reason she did not understand her unease remained.

"I am indebted to her, sir," Jenna replied, glancing round at the opulence of the furnishings.

"Would you care for some supper?" he invited, shuffling towards a table set out with a cold collation. All the dishes looked delicious but Jenna did not feel in the least like eating but was afraid of offending this man and ruining her chances of obtaining a post in his household.

Mr Quint sat opposite her and helped to serve the food. Jenna noted that he ate little himself but seemed excited. "Do have some wine, my dear," he urged. "It is quite exceptional."

"No, really. . . ."

Despite her refusal he poured a glassful although his hand shook ever so slightly. He filled his own and raised it, "To a fruitful association."

Reluctant as she was and unused to alcohol, nevertheless Jenna raised her glass. As he drained his she did so too. The liquid felt as though it burned her throat and immeidately her head began to reel.

"Are you all right?" he asked, displaying concern as he peered at her through the gloom.

She contrived to smile, not wishing to appear a fool. "Oh yes, indeed, sir."

He was immediately reassured and she said in a conver- esational tone, "It was my great fortune to encounter Mrs Creevy this morning."

Mr Quint licked his lips. "No greater than mine, my dear. Mrs Creevy told me you arrived in Town only today."

He looked at her speculatively and she answered, "Yes, that is quite true."

Her answer made him beam. "That is splendid, quite

splendid. If you have finished, we may get down to the . . . er business in hand."

He held her chair as she got to her feet and then moved towards the sofa. When they were seated, he uncomfortably near, she said, "I believe your wife is a chronic invalid."

"Ah yes." He looked mournful. "It is a great sorrow to me, my dear. Can you blame a man finding pleasure where he may?"

"No . . . no, I dare say not."

He edged even closer and she asked, feeling a mite discomforted, "Do you think I will be suitable, sir?"

"Oh yes, indeed, my dear. I do so like young country girls, so fresh, so clean. Oh yes indeed. You are eminently suitable."

Jenna looked at him in consternation as he licked his lips again. He raised his hand to touch her hair. "So pretty," he murmured.

Alarmed Jenna jerked her head away from him. Her head swam again which seemed odd as she had drunk only one glass of wine. She put one hand to her head and Mr Quint's face loomed grotesquely in front of her.

"I think . . . I am . . . unwell," she gasped.

"Here, allow me to help you," he offered, putting his arms around her. " 'Tis nothing."

His breath was hot on her cheek and such intimacy from a stranger was abhorrent to her. However, freeing herself from his unwanted embrace was not so easy as all strength seemed to have left her body.

"Mr Quint," she gasped. "I beg of you remember propriety."

His reply was to laugh. "Such spirit," he murmured as she struggled anew.

Again she tried to tell him she was ill but he was too intent upon clasping her to him in a clumsy, bruising way.

Suddenly he pressed his lips against hers and Jenna, panic-stricken, began to pummel him. He seemed enormously strong and her struggling was to no avail. She tried to scream but no sound issued from her lips. Her hand vainly sought some way of making him stop and in doing so she knocked off his tasselled cap, but that did not stop the bruising assault on her body.

Suddenly her fingers located a hard, cold object on a table nearby. Jenna gasped again and raised it, bringing it hard down on his head. Mr Quint cried out and slid away from her at last, slowly down onto the floor. For a long moment Jenna could feel only relief, but then she recalled what she had done. When she dared to look he was lying senseless on the floor and there was a gash on the side of his head from which blood was seeping. Jenna found she was holding a cut-glass dish, its jagged edges stained with the blood and hair of Mr Quint. Realising what she had done she let go of the dish and it fell to the floor to smash into a thousand pieces.

"I've killed him," she cried, her eyes wide with terror.

Beside herself with fear and grief she began to sob as the sound of pounding footsteps came even nearer. Jenna couldn't take her eyes off the inert form of Mr Quint and she became aware that blood was slowly staining the hem of her once pristine gown.

The door flew open and the room was flooded with light from the branches of candles held aloft by two servants. They rushed into the room and then were arrested by the scene before them.

"Cor!" cried one of the footmen, "The jade's put an end to Mr Quint!"

"No no!" she cried. "It was not my fault."

"You'll pay for this, you jade!" cried the other as Jenna covered her face with her hands and sobbed heartbrokenly.

31

FOUR

It was dusk when a carriage drew up close to a side-entrance to Newgate Prison, a grim castellated building the sight of which sent shivers down the spines of even law-abiding people.

No escutcheon decorated the doors of the carriage and leather curtains were drawn across the windows. When the carriage came to a halt a young man enveloped in an all-embracing cloak stepped down and then turned back to address the only other occupant.

"Mama, stay here. I shall go inside myself. Newgate is no place for such as you."

Harriet Fordyce was already climbing down. She too was enveloped in a cloak, the hood covering her dark hair. "Tush, Gerald. This task is too important to be entrusted entirely to you."

Her son gave a gasp of exasperation. "Mama! Really!"

"The slightest error at this point and the plan is finished before it is even begun. There is nowhere else we can go after this place. The orphan asylums and the other prisons haven't yielded anyone remotely suited to our purpose."

He drew in a deep breath. "Very well; if you insist upon it, Mama."

32

"I do. Now hurry. We have no time to lose. We must not tarry here longer than necessary. Lead the way."

The turnkey was waiting at the door with a lantern. He grinned in anticipation when he saw the visitors and bowed low before them.

"You have received my instructions?" Gerald asked, looking at the man with disdain.

"Yes, yer lordship. This way, if you please. You'll 'ave to 'urry. Wouldn't do to be found 'ere, would it now?"

"You may be very certain we shall remain here no longer than absolutely necessary," the young man replied.

Still grinning the turnkey led them along corridors which echoed with the cries, moans and even laughter of the inmates. Hands reached out through the bars to clutch at their clothes. Gerald looked at all the hapless creatures with alarm and his mother pulled her cloak more tightly around her as if it might serve as some form of protection.

" 'Elp a poor soul, m'lord," came a plaintive cry as they passed by.

"You've got to get me out of here!" screamed another.

A once glamorous harridan posed against the bars thrusting her hand out to delay Gerald Fordyce. "Fancy me, yer lordship. Get me out and you won't be disappointed."

His face bore a look of distaste. The stench was appalling and he held a perfumed handkerchief close to his nose.

"This is where yer want to be." The turnkey slipped his giant key into a lock and the gate swung open. Gerald hesitated before preceding him inside, followed by his mother.

"Gad, what a hell-hole this is," he cried, looking around at the ragged and filthy creatures who were once women.

"Got no money to do more for 'em, m'lord," the turnkey answered apologetically. "B'sides, a rascally murderin' lot they are, all o'em. Watch yer purse, yer lordship, or they'll 'ave it off yer quicker than 'ell can scorch a feather, beggin' yer pardon, ma'am."

A dozen cronies rushed up to them, but the turnkey fended them off roughly and lit the way across the cell. The two visitors picked their way carefully, avoiding those creatures too far gone in their misery even to get up to inspect the newcomers. Harriet Fordyce kept close to her son and held her cloak about her face.

"This is the one yer after, yer lordship," the turnkey told Gerald, holding up his lantern so that they could see the better.

Both Gerald and his mother gazed down at the pitiful creature who stared up at them blankly with red-rimmed eyes. Her dark hair hung in thin wisps down her filthy face.

The young man gave a gasp of exasperation. "I did say fair hair, jailer, and it has to be someone very young."

"Only five and twenty, this one, yer lordship, but I'll grant she looks older. Bein' in 'ere tends to 'ave a bad effect on them. Grieves me something shocking, it does."

"Well, she won't do," Harriet reiterated. "Moreover we want a girl who hasn't been here long enough to be brutalised by her circumstances." She glanced around. "These creatures are too far gone."

Gerald put one weary hand up to his face. "What *are* we to do now? I had pinned all my hopes on this. There is nowhere left to go."

The turnkey looked suddenly shifty as he stroked his unshaven chin. "Might just 'ave the one yer after, yer lordship."

"Why did you not take us to her immediately, instead of wasting our time?" Gerald said in exasperation.

"There is a problem with that one, yer lordship. She's accounted for, if yer know what I mean."

Hands were clawing at their clothes. Gerald closed his

fingers over his purse and with the other hand freed himself from the importuning old crone.

"No, I don't now what you mean, but you may explain to us outside."

He glanced around him before leading his mother to the gate. The turnkey let them out, saying, "It's like this, yer lordship; this one's for the hulks—transportation to the Colonies, and she's on the list. She'll be missed if I let 'er go, but there's a remedy, there is. It'll just cost more money."

Mrs Fordyce gasped with exasperation and spoke at last. "How will that solve the problem? If she will be missed there is nought anyone can do."

"The extra money can pay for another to take 'er place," the jailer replied.

"What manner of creature would possibly do so?" Gerald asked scornfully.

"Plenty willin', yer lordship. Oh yes, some'll even go to the Colonies to get out of this place."

"I can easily understand why," Gerald answered with feeling as hands reached out through the bars all around them. "Very well, I'm persuaded an arrangement can be made . . ."

"Eh?" asked the jailer.

Gerald gasped. "I shall pay *if* the creature you have in mind is suitable."

The fellow looked shifty once again. "For what, I'm bound to ask?"

"That doesn't concern you," the young man snapped. "Show us the way. We have no wish to tarry here longer than necessary."

As the man hurried to unlock the gate to another cell, Gerald said softly to his mother, "I'll warrant this one will be useless too."

35

"Oh, do not say so, for it is out last opportunity, and so much is at stake."

Once again several filthy crones rushed up to them to be pushed away. Both visitors stared in horror at the filthy and ragged children who ran up to them, hands outstretched. "Oh, my God!" Harried Fordyce cried. "Children."

"Came with their mothers," the jailer explained. "Don't encourage them, ma'am. They'll take the skin off yer backs, given half a chance."

Ignoring the fellow Mrs Fordyce said, "Gerald, give them something," shuddering as she did so.

"Murderin' bitches," cried the jailer, pushing his way through a mass of importuning hands. Gerald Fordyce distributed a few coins and then ushered his mother to where the turnkey was waiting for them.

Several women were huddled in straw, some were writhing mutely on the bare floor, clad only in filthy and torn shifts.

"My God," Gerald whispered, "I hope all this is going to be worth the effort."

"It will," his mother promised.

"If we do not have our throats slit first."

"If you have no stomach for this say so now and wait five years to share with Hollingdale what is rightfully yours," she told him in a harsh whisper.

"Point taken, Mama."

The turnkey was standing in the corner, holding up his lantern once again. "Real gentry mort, this one, yer lordship. If that's what yer after."

Gerald Fordyce looked down at the creature huddled into a pile of filthy straw, her once white evening gown torn, filthy and stained with blood. A mane of golden curls tumbled to her bare shoulders and a pair of deep blue eyes gazed fearfully up at them.

Mrs Fordyce drew in a sharp breath. "What is your name, child?"

She didn't answer and the turnkey jabbed at her with the toe of his boot. "Jenna . . . Jenna . . . Tregail," she answered at last.

Gerald Fordyce looked at the jailer who said, "What did I tell yer? Proper Quality, she is."

"What did she do?" the young man asked, looking back to the girl who shrank further into the straw.

One of the other women did a little dance ending with the travesty of a curtsey. "Proper lady she thinks she is even though she's a murderin' bitch just like the rest o'us."

"Murder!" Gerald exclaimed, his eyes growing wide.

"All o'em in 'ere 'ave killed someone," the turnkey explained, "or nearly. Most o'em are for the gibbet afore long." He laughed as the two visitors drew in sharp breaths. "Caved in the 'ead of a gentry cove, this one did. Near as killed 'im, the jade. Wouldn't think so to look at 'er, would yer, m'lord?"

"Is that true?" Gerald asked of the girl in a harsh voice.

She averted her fear-filled eyes from his. "It wasn't . . . my . . . fault. He tried to . . ."

Tears began to slide down her cheeks just when she thought there were no more tears left to cry.

Gerald looked at his mother. "Mama, what do you think?"

The woman had not taken her attention from Jenna since they set eyes upon her. "She'll do when she's cleaned up. She's better than I ever dared to hope after our fruitless search."

The turnkey's eyes narrowed. "Goin' to cost yer, y'know. This one's down for the 'ulks."

"No!" Jenna cried. "It isn't fair. I didn't mean any harm, only he wouldn't stop! I didn't mean to hurt anyone!"

Gerald Fordyce handed the turnkey his purse. "I belive this should cover the cost of a replacement."

When he opened the purse the man's eyes grew wide. "Yes, yer lordship. Oh, yes!"

Harriet bent down and tired to get Jenna to stand up. "Come along, my dear. You're coming with us."

Jenna drew back, her eyes filled with terror. "Where . . . where are you taking me?"

"Out of here."

"Did Mrs Creevy send you?"

"No, I know no one of that name. Come along now. We have delayed long enough."

She pulled Jenna to her feet and, seeing the torn and flimsy gown, ordered, "Gerald, give this girl your cloak."

At first he hesitated but then cast it over the girl's shoulders with a flourish. Jenna, despite her fear and hesitation, clutched it around her gratefully. "I am a convicted felon," she stammered. "You cannot take me out of here."

"It has all been arranged," Mrs Fordyce told her in a soothing tone. "Don't you wish to escape this dreadful prison?"

"Yes, but . . ."

The other woman looked at the turnkey and ordered, "Lead the way out of here."

Once again Jenna pulled back and another woman rushed forward. "Take me in her stead. I'll go. I'll go anywhere with you. I beg of you to take me . . ."

The turnkey pushed her roughly to one side, at the same time as taking Jenna's arm and pulling her towards the gate. The two visitors hurried after.

"Take hold of her, Gerald," his mother ordered when the jailer locked the gate in the faces of the others who were pressed close to the bars.

38

Gerald put his arm around Jenna's trembling shoulders and manoeuvred the less than willing girl along the corridor as quickly as they could go.

"Where are we going?" she asked in bewilderment, stumbling along in his wake. "Who *are* you? Where are you taking me?"

The door to the prison closed behind them and Mrs Fordyce took a deep breath of air before replying, "I am Harriet Fordyce and this is my son, Gerald." He nodded affably and Mrs Fordyce went on, "We are taking you to safety, warmth and food. I am persuaded you will appreciate all three."

They bundled her into the carriage and immediately the door was closed it set off at a spanking pace. Jenna huddled into the corner looking at them properly for the first time, the handsome buck and the elegant woman in black.

"I hope I shall never see the inside of that hell-hole again," Gerald declared in heartfelt tones.

"Why did you rescue me?" Jenna demanded, her eyes wide with fear.

The other woman smiled reassuringly. "My dear, you have suffered a terrible ordeal. First you must rest, eat and bathe. Then the explanations will begin, and all will be made clear to you."

"I have been in London such a short time and yet one thing I have learned is that there are precious few benefactors."

Gerald smiled then. "My dear, we are not that."

"You paid the turnkey to release me."

"It is hoped you will render us a service in return. It will be of mutual benefit I assure you."

Jenna shivered. "Like Mr Quint I suppose."

"Mr Quint?" Gerald enquired. "Who may he be?"

"The man I . . . almost killed."

39

"Ah yes, we must not forget your crime." He smiled again. "You need not fear; I rather believe you will not find our proposition distasteful."

Jenna continued to look suspicious but for now anything was better than Newgate. The fresh night air was something she had never valued before, but it smelled so sweet now although no more so than the freedom from the cries and howls which were continuous in the prison. It was impossible to sleep because of the cold, hunger and noise in there. If anyone did manage to sleep there was the danger of having the clothes stolen off one's back. Even now Jenna could scarcely believe it had all happened to her and was not a hideous nightmare.

The carriage slowed to a stop and Jenna tensed again. "Where are we?" she asked, trying to peer out of the curtained windows.

"My house," Gerald Fordyce answered. "You will find it more comfortable than Newgate."

He laughed and she stared at him in horror. His mother smiled reassuringly. "Don't let my son tease you, dear. You are perfectly safe with us."

Gerald Fordyce climbed down and then helped both ladies out of the carriage. Jenna was hurried inside between them and then immediately up the stairs. She had no time to evaluate her surroundings, but the house did seem both spacious and luxurious like Mrs Creevy's, so Jenna was no more reassured.

Gerald Fordyce relinquished his hold on her only when his mother took her into a bedchamber and closed the door. Warmth from a roaring fire met them. Heavy brocade curtains shrouded the windows and there were just enough candles to afford a gentle light. Mrs Fordyce led Jenna towards the fire and removed the cloak, easing the girl into a chair.

"There. Just sit quietly, my dear and I shall send for some food and water. You will wish to bathe, I have no doubt."

"I don't believe I shall ever be clean again," Jenna replied, too weary to be on her guard any longer.

Just then she was too tired and too dispirited to question any further. It hardly mattered just at that moment the reason for their kindness. Nothing could be worse than Newgate and it was enough to be free of the smells and sounds of that place.

A maid arrived soon afterwards and Mrs Fordyce gave her explicit instructions. The maid cast Jenna a curious look before hurrying away again. Harriet Fordyce came back across the room to find Jenna staring sightlessly into space.

"I am sensible of the fact that you cannot think to trust us as yet . . ." she began.

"It is no reflection upon you, ma'am. I shall never be able to trust anyone again."

Harriet Fordyce smiled uncomfortably. "I wish you would believe we mean you no harm, quite the contrary, but tomorrow, after you have rested, is soon enough to explain."

Jenna looked up at her. "Do you have no qualms about harbouring a convicted felon beneath your roof?"

Again the woman looked uncomfortable. "My dear, you declared your innocence and as a keen judge of character I believed you."

An army of servants arrived with food, clothing, a bath and water. Mrs Fordyce withdrew, leaving a maid to attend her guest. Jenna luxuriated in the hot scented water and allowed the maid to wash her matted curls. The rags which were once her gown and shift were taken away and a soft lawn nightgown laid out for her.

A selection of cold meats and puddings had been put out on a table and, feeling refreshed from her bath, Jenna ate heartily for the first time in days. No wine had been put out, to her relief, and she welcomed the rich taste of the chocolate poured for her by the maid-servant. When she had eaten her fill, the maid cleared away the dishes and withdrew, leaving Jenna to herself at last.

It was then that she walked across to the window and pulled back the heavy curtains to peer out at an elegant square surrounded by beautifully appointed houses. As she stood there a carriage drew up outside the house. Gerald Fordyce stepped out of the front door, addressed a comment to an unseen lackey and, dressed for the evening, climbed into the carriage.

When it set off again she allowed the curtain to drop back into place, feeling all at once weary. She couldn't recall when she had last slept properly—at Mrs Creevy's—and that was a long time ago. The bed was inviting but Jenna had become very wary of sleep, something which remained with her. Suddenly, though, she could no longer keep her eyes open. Sleep was creeping up on her remorselessly and she found herself staggering towards the bed where she fell into an immediate and deep slumber.

FIVE

Fingers dragged at Jenna's clothes, pulling them from her body. Chains dragged her down, preventing her from defending herself from the assault. A grotesque and distorted face loomed in front of her and she recognised it as Mr Quint's.

"You will be transported to the Colonies for seven years," he intoned.

"No, no," she cried.

His face began to run with blood and she cried out again, trying to shut out the image unsuccessfully.

"Jenna! Jenna, wake up."

Someone was shaking her. Jenna opened her eyes and cried out before she saw it was Harriet Fordyce leaning over her. Once again the woman was wearing a black gown.

"You're safe. Do you not recall?"

Jenna gasped and brushed back her hair. "Yes, yes, I remember."

Mrs Fordyce looked sympathetic. "You were having a bad dream, I think."

Jenns's eyes clouded with remembrance. "Since arriving in London my life has been a very long nightmare."

The woman sat down on the edge of the bed. "That is all

43

ended now, my dear. Your fortunes from now on are changing for the better.''

Jenna looked unconvinced. Harriet Fordyce leaned forward to lift a cup of chocolate from the bedside table. "Drink this, Jenna. It will make you feel better and then when you are dressed you can take breakfast with us downstairs. My son is very taken with you and is longing to speak with you."

She thrust the cup in front of Jenna's face which made her laugh. "No, I thank you. I drank enough chocolate last night. It certainly made me sleep deeply, if not well.''

"You needed something to make you sleep last night. I assure you this is pure chocolate."

She handed Jenna the cup and then got to her feet, walking towards the door. "I have brought you a gown to wear. When you're dressed come downstairs and join us. We'll be waiting for you.''

The moment she had gone Jenna put the cup down and swung her legs over the side of the bed. Mrs Fordyce had left a wine-coloured velvet gown on the end of the bed.

It was as fashionable as the one Mrs Creevy had given her, but far more modest. Jenna clung onto one of the bedposts and laid her head against it. Beads of perspiration broke out on her brow. What did they want with her? she wondered. Was everyone in London up to mischief? It certainly seemed as if they were.

Hot water had been left in the washstand bowl. Jenna splashed some on her face to dispel the last of the drugged sleep and quickly put on the gown which fitted well. The cloak was still where Mrs Fordyce had left it the night before. Jenna tossed it over the gown and hurried to the door. She peered out of a crack and then, when the corridor appeared deserted, she slipped out, hurrying as fast as she could without making any noise.

44

She hesitated on the landing, feeling faint with fear; good fortune was with her and the hall was deserted, much to her relief. She hurried down the stairs, all the while afraid someone would appear. She was halfway across the seemingly endless hall, moving towards the door, when Gerald Fordyce came out of the one of the downstairs rooms.

"Ah, there you are, Miss Tregail." Jenna's head reeled and her mouth was dry. Tears of frustration pricked at her eyes. "It is Miss Tregail, is it not?"

His smile was an ironic one and feeling foolish and more than a little afraid she answered, "Yes, that is my name."

He was very elegantly dressed in a broad-shouldered coat of dark blue superfine, skin-tight pantaloons and a lawn shirt, the collar points of which were so high they allowed him to turn his head with only the greatest difficulty.

He came forward and she flinched away when he reached out to touch her, but he merely removed the cloak. With it, it seemed, he removed her last chance of escape. "Mama is waiting for you, Miss Tregail."

Firmly but gently he took her arm and led her into a spacious dining-room where Harriet Fordyce was seated at a mahogany table. Silver chafing dishes and fine china graced the table which was large enough to accommodate a dozen or more people.

The woman smiled when she saw Jenna. "Miss Tregail, you look quite a different person this morning."

"Indeed," her son concurred. "I scarce recognised her."

"Do join us for some breakfast, my dear."

Gerald escorted her to a chair near his mother and rather reluctantly she sat down. After that he walked around the table and sat down to face Jenna, smiling faintly.

"Mis Tregail was about to take a breath of air, Mama," he told her, still smiling.

"I can well understand your need to do so, my dear, and after breakfast if you so wish we shall walk together in the garden." She leaned forward as her son began to help himself from the various dishes. "We were wondering if there was anyone . . . a relative . . . you wish to advise of your safety."

Jenna stared sightlessly past her, a tide of hopelessness washing over her. "No. There is no one."

"How unusual," Gerald commented, his mouth full of eggs. "Have you recently become orphaned?"

"Long ago and my cousin in Penzance is not interested in my well-being. There is no one else."

As Mrs Fordyce exchanged a significant look with her son Jenna realised she had been foolish in making such an admission, but it was too late to be sorry. It was done.

"Poor child," Mrs Fordyce crooned and then, "What will you have to eat?"

Jenna's hand clenched into a fist on top of the table. "Nothing. I want nothing except to know what all this is about."

"After breakfast we shall talk," Gerald Fordyce promised.

"I'm not hungry."

"You must be," Gerald contradicted, his mouth full of food. "The kidneys are quite delicious."

Jenna shot him a hate-filled look as his mother said, "You really mustn't be afraid of us, my dear. We intend you no harm. Indeed we shall improve your situation."

"Ever since I arrived in London people have been exceeding kind to me," she answered, her tone uncharacteristically bitter, "but only for their own evil ends. First Mrs Creevy and then Mr Quint. You must forgive me if I cannot bring myself to believe you."

Gerald stopped eating and stared at her in astonishment. "Did you say Mrs *Creevy*?"

Jenna looked away. "She met me at the staging inn when I arrived and promised to introduce me to a prospective employer, Mr Quint. It was he . . . ."

Her mind shied away from the memory of the terrible evening, but she started with shock when Gerald, dabbing his lips with the napkin, began to laugh.

"Mrs *Creevy*?"

"Yes," Jenna replied indignantly.

"Oh, my goodness, what a lark! You speak of the infamous Ida Creevy, I'll be bound. Ida Creevy. You must have been nursed in cotton to believe her Banbury Tales, my dear."

His mother looked as bewildered as Jenna. "Do you know this woman, Gerald?"

"Half the bucks in London do, Mama. She runs a rather high-priced bawdy-house not far from Covent Garden. Devilishly handy, I must admit. It is her habit, I am told, to haunt staging inns to meet young, friendless girls just up from the country."

Jenna's eyes grew wide as the truth of the matter dawned upon her at last. How foolish she had been. What a green girl to believe in that woman's benevolence. "Then there could not have been a situation as companion to Mr Quint's wife!"

Gerald laughed again. "No indeed! He had quite another purpose in mind."

Jenna's hand crept to her throat. "What a chuckle-head I have been."

Harriet Fordyce cast her a sympathetic look. "Did no one warn you of these creatures who lie in wait for the innocent?" Jenna shook her head and the other woman went on, "Was it this Mr Quint you attacked?"

"It was so unfair. His servants who gave evidence against me were biased. They didn't know I was only protecting myself, but the judge wouldn't believe me."

"I see," Mrs Fordyce breathed. "It is all apparent now, but what a catalogue of misfortune."

Gerald Fordyce had resumed eating his breakfast by then and commented, "It is a relief to know we are not harbouring a desperate rapscallion beneath our roof. It would be devilishly awkward if we were obliged to be on our guard for fear you might slit out throats."

Jenna stiffened and Mrs Fordyce laughed. "It was evident to me last night that Mrs Tregail was no felon."

"Your anxieties might well have been allayed, Mr Fordyce, but mine remain," Jenna pointed out.

The other woman pushed away her plate. "It is indeed time we explained our reasons for rescuing you from your awful fate, undeserved as it was. It was not solely a humanitarian act . . ."

Jenna laughed harshly. "I did not think it would be. When I arrived in London I was but a green girl. I believed every one to be good and kind, just like most of those I had always known. What happened to me since has changed my opinions entirely. I am no longer a chaw-bacon, and I trust no one."

"And with very good reason," Mrs Fordyce agreed while her son looked amused. "Let me explain and you will see you have nothing to fear from us." She glanced at her son who was again enjoying his breakfast and seeming unconcerned with the conversation around him. "A short while ago my brother, John Ransome, died, much to our sorrow. He was very wealthy and left no direct heirs to his estate. Well, it seemed as if it was so, for his wife passed away in childbirth and his daughter, Annabel, died when she was only three or four years of age. I cannot quite recall her exact age."

48

Jenna looked at her wide-eyed and uncomprehending, and after a momentary pause the woman continued, "Gerald was always close to his uncle, as close as it was possible to be, for the tragic events in his life affected him somewhat. He acted in a strange manner for much of the time but my son fully expected to be named as sole heir to the estate. However, it appears my brother believed his child to be still alive and has named her his heir, if she can be found. If not, in no sooner than five years, Gerald shares the estate with his cousin, Charles. It is an iniquitous situation, you must agree."

Jenna continued to look bewildered. "What has all this to do with me?"

"There is no doubt little Annabel died in the river and was swept out to sea, but Gerald does not wish to wait five years to share an estate which is rightfully his with his rascally cousin who, in truth, is not deserving of a single penny. If Annabel is discovered to be alive then the matter can be resolved soon rather than in five years time, and to Gerald's satisfaction."

"I still cannot conceive what that is to do with me," Jenna insisted.

Gerald dabbed at his lips again. "My dear girl, you are to be Annabel come back from the dead."

She shrank back in the high-backed chair. "Oh no. I couldn't . . . How could I? I know nothing about her . . . her life . . . her family."

A smile played about the lips of the other woman. "Do you not realise, Miss Tregail, if Annabel were alive she would know nothing of her life at Barnston Manor. She was no more than a babe when she disappeared."

"How could you explain away her absence?" Jenna then asked.

"Quite easily," Mrs Fordyce replied. "At the time she

disappeared it was at first thought she might have been abducted by gypsies who were known to be in the area. We would concoct a story on these lines and no one could possibly prove it untrue."

Jenna slowly got to her feet, gripping the back of the chair until her knuckles were white. "You couldn't possibly arrive with me and declare me your niece. It would look far too suspicious."

Mrs Fordyce laughed softly again. "We are not so cork-brained to attempt such a thing. Gerald and I have thought on this matter carefully for some time. We have studied the problems and pitfalls which we believe can be overcome. Naturally, it cannot be seen we have any connection with you. Our servants here are loyal and the rascally turnkey at Newgate will not betray his own corrupt little schemes."

Gerald's cup chinked in its saucer and he cleared his throat. "Some years ago my late father granted a band of tinkers the right to camp over the winter in one of his fields. They still do so and it is time they repaid his generosity. It is they who will be tempted by the generous reward being offered for Annabel's return. When you arrive Mama and I will be as surprised as everyone else—and, I may warn you, as suspicious. After all I shall be the loser when Annabel returns so I cannot be suspected of any connection with her arrival."

"You will surely need more proof of my identity than the word of a tinker," Jenna pointed out. "I cannot suddenly present myself as Annabel Ransome and expect to be accepted without question."

"How many gypsies have golden hair?" Gerald pointed out.

Harriet Fordyce slipped a chain over her head. Attached to it was a gold locket. She handed it to Jenna who, with trembling fingers, opened it. Inside were two miniature portraits, a dark-haired autocratic young man, and a fair-haired woman with a sweet half-smile.

"My brother and sister-in-law," Mrs Fordyce informed her. "The miniatures were painted at the time of their marriage, which was just as well for within a year my poor sister-in-law was dead. Not long afterwards Jack gave me the locket as a keepsake. He is now dead and I do not suppose anyone knows I have it. There is your proof, in addition," she smiled, "to one or two other little refinements which we can discuss later."

Jenna left the locket on the table and walked slowly to the window. "This is all very well, but if you do succeed, *I* shall inherit the Ransome legacy which will not help Mr Fordyce. I can scarce hand it over without my generosity causing some suspicion."

She heard the scrape of chair legs on the floor and then became aware that Gerald Fordyce was walking across the room towards her as she gazed out onto a pretty, walled garden. Somewhere beyond it a pedlar was calling her wares.

She started when he rested his hands on her shoulders. "The simple answer," he said in a gentle voice, "is for you and I to me married whereupon your property becomes mine, inviting no suspicion."

She whirled round then, her eyes wide and disbelieving. "Marry you!"

He laughed while his mother looked on anxiously. "You looked absolutely horrified, Miss Tregail. Is it so unthinkable? Am I such an ogre? Or mayhap repulsive to you?"

His mockery made her avert her eyes. "I beg your pardon, sir. I didn't intend to insult you, only the suggestion came as a shock after everything else that has happened of late."

"You are far too blunt," his mother said.

51

"I do beg your forgiveness, Miss Tregail, but time is too short for a lengthy debate on the subject. You must own we should make a handsome pair when the time arrives."

Unable to bear him so close to her any longer Jenna walked slowly away, and as she did so he added, "Do not concern yourself on the matter. We shall come to an amicable arrangement. Many men become leg-shackled to heiresses far less fetching than you, and I shall not make too many demands upon your time. When the estate is finally settled there will be a choice of houses where you can live apart from Barnston Manor. If you so desire we need meet on only a few occasions."

"Gerald," his mother admonished, "it is all so far ahead of you and this has all been a great shock to Miss Tregail. You must not tease her."

He looked suddenly bitter. "You would think after Newgate and the threat of transportation Miss Tregail would fairly welcome the notion. I'm of the opinion any one of the creatures sharing her cell would do so with alacrity."

"I do not regard myself as a felon," Jenna retorted sharply.

"Nevertheless the law says that is what you are."

Jenna put one hand to her head which was reeling. "I'm persuaded if I do not agree to this crack-brained scheme I will very quickly find myself back in Newgate."

Mrs Fordyce laughed disparagingly. "My dear girl, I cannot conceive why you should think so."

"Nonsense, Mama," her son scoffed. "If Miss Tregail does not co-operate with us what else are we to do with her?"

His mother cast him a warning look. "I confess it would be inconvenient to have to seek out another, not to say expensive, but after all we are offering you a splendid opportunity, one any young lady might seize with alacrity, let alone one as penniless and friendless as you."

Jenna went to sit down at the table again, staring into space. She knew then that she would die rather than go back to the hell of Newgate or slavery in the Colonies. She had heard tales of the heat, the dirt and disease. Transportation for one such as she was a virtual death sentence. At least with the Fordyces whom she still did not trust, there was always a chance of eventual freedom. She glanced up at Gerald Fordyce whom she loathed despite his handsome features and fashionably languid air. Even marriage to him could not be worse.

"I shall do as you wish," she answered at last and Mrs Fordyce glanced triumphantly at her son. "Now, may I have some breakfast?"

SIX

"The beef is excellent," Mr Pritchett commented as he pushed another forkful into his mouth. "Your housekeeper is exceptional."

Harriet Fordyce smiled at him across the table. "Mrs Tarrand is indeed a fine housekeeper, I own. My brother was always fortunate in his servants. His cook, as you now realise, is superior to most."

Gerald Fordyce sat back in his chair in the dining-room at Barnston Manor. He smiled encouragingly at the pretty maidservant who was hovering nearby, exhibiting her nervousness. One of the footmen spoke to her sharply and she took up a tray and hurried from the room.

"Who is the new maidservant, Mama?" he enquired as she left the room. His gaze followed her until the door was shut.

Mrs Fordyce glanced around. "Mrs Tarrand's niece. She needed extra help and the girl was in want of employment. I understand her mother recently expired and Mrs Tarrand feels somewhat responsible for her."

"She does not resemble her aunt in the slightest," the young man mused, reaching for his wineglass, "which is a mercy."

"When one reaches my age, Mr Fordyce," the lawyer observed, "one wishes only for good and loyal service."

"There is no reason why that cannot be combined with a handsome countenance," Gerald pointed out.

"Oh, quite so," the lawyer agreed.

From beneath the lowered lids Gerald Fordyce observed the lawyer as he ate. There was a faint smile playing about the corners of his lips. Momentarily he glanced at the bracket clock on the mantel before taking up his fork and murmuring, "Uncle Jack was not so fortunate in his choice of nursery-maid. As I recall it was her negligence which resulted in the . . . er . . . loss of my cousin."

The lawyer shook his head. "Shocking business, Mr Fordyce. Your uncle was quite undone afterwards. I have dealt with a great many people in my career, but I have never seen a man change so radically, and it was understandable too. To lose a wife and child in so short a time is indeed shocking. I suppose you have invited me here to give an account of the search for your cousin."

"That and for you, as executor, to ascertain the estate is being run correctly."

"In the absence of my nephew," Mrs Fordyce broke in, "Gerald believed it incumbent upon himself to call in at Barnston Manor from time to time to ascertain all is in order."

"Quite so," the lawyer agreed, helping himself to another portion of beef. "I am persuaded that Major Hollingdale himself would agree." He looked up briefly. "Has anyone heard from that young man of late?"

Gerald Fordyce chuckled softly. "That was precisely the question I was about to put to you, sir."

Mr Pritchett shook his head. "I have, of course, written to him, but communications are not of the most efficient in the Peninsula."

"My nephew is such a hothead," Mrs Fordyce observed " 'tis a wonder he is still alive. The last we heard he was on the personal staff of Sir John Moore."

"No doubt we shall have word in due course. He cannot claim his share of the estate for some time to come so it is of no account." The lawyer frowned. "As I recall Mr Hollingdale was a rather charming young fellow with great style."

"Oh, indeed," Mrs Fordyce agreed wryly. "Only he is now Major Hollingdale."

"Yes, indeed, I recall. Wouldn't have thought that young man a soldier of the King, no more than . . ." He was looking at Gerald and his voice died away in embarrassment.

"My cousin was always eminently suited to fighting," the young man responded, "having had a good deal of practice before he joined the army. Even so it is more like he is doing so in the bawdy-houses of the Peninsula than the battlefields."

"Quite so." The lawyer looked uncomfortable. "We cannot all lead blameless lives, more's the pity." He cleared his throat and waved his fork in the air. "I can tell you notices have been placed in journals the length and breadth of the country in search for Miss Ransome."

Once again Gerald sat back in his chair. For once his dinner was scarcely touched. "If my cousin is still alive, which all of us doubt, it is like she was abducted by gypsies and it is rare that they can read let alone indulge in the luxury of buying journals."

Mr Pritchett smiled at him pityingly as the lackey refilled the wineglasses. "My dear Mr Fordyce, where money is concerned I can assure you the gypsies the length and breadth of this fair land will come to hear of it."

Gerald glanced at the clock once again and shifted

uneasily in his chair. His mother followed the direction of his gaze as the servants removed the dishes and replaced them with those containing the puddings.

"Ah, syllabub," Mr Pritchett observed gleefully, clapping his hands together as the dishes were set down. "And apple tart. Someone has purposely produced my favourite puddings."

Harriet Fordyce's eyes met those of her son's who looked heavenward. A moment later he took out his gold hunter and checked the time against that on the bracket clock.

"A few days in the country is very welcome," the lawyer remarked as he partook of a generous portion of syllabub washed down by more wine. He looked to his host and hostess in bewilderment. "Do you not wish to join me in this delicious repast?"

Mrs Fordyce started guiltily and then smiled, a trifle sadly. "I'm afraid my brother's sudden passing still affects us, Mr Pritchett. Gerald and I were uncommonly devoted to him."

"Oh, indeed." The lawyer returned his attention to the pudding whilst mother and son were exchanging anxious looks. However, a few moments later the door opened and both of them looked across the room, their expressions reflecting their eagerness and alarm.

The house-steward walked in with maddening slowness, looking directly at Harriet Fordyce. "An . . . er . . . gentleman is here to see you, ma'am."

The woman looked outraged. "At this time? What nonsense."

"I have explained that the family is at dinner, ma'am, but the . . . gentleman insists the matter is of great import."

"Who is it?" Gerald asked, affecting irritation.

"He says his name is Bill Smith, sir."

"I have never heard of the fellow," Mrs Fordyce replied, appearing to be outraged. "Has he got a card?"

"No, ma'am, but he does say it has something to do with the reward that's being offered for Miss Annabel."

At this Pritchett stopped eating and looked up. "Is he by any chance a gypsy?"

"Yes, sir, it would appear he is of that type."

All three of them were on their feet immediately. Mrs Fordyce went to her son and held his arm. The lawyer waited for them to precede him from the room.

"It will no doubt be a nonsense," Mr Pritchett said, "but we must see the fellow."

"Oh indeed," the younger man responded, trying hard to hide his smile.

It appeared the house-steward had left the caller in the hall rather than showing him into the drawing-room, as was the normal practice with visitors. The gypsy was an unshaven, filthy-looking man, who appeared ill at ease in his unfamiliar surroundings.

"There won't be no trouble will there?" he asked, his eyes shifty and narrow, the moment he saw them.

"No, no, you have nothing to fear," Mr Pritchett assured him. "Come along in here where we may discuss the matter in private."

The gypsy took off his battered hat and handed it to the obviously outraged house-steward. The lawyer then ushered the man into the drawing-room and when Mrs Fordyce sat down Mr Pritchett asked, "I gather you might have information about a Miss Annabel Ransome."

The gypsy continued to look uneasy as he perched on the edge of an elegant brocaded bergere chair.

"I'll wager it will be a tissue of lies," Gerald protested. " 'Tis evident the man's a mountebank."

"Let us hear what you have to say, Mr Smith," the lawyer insisted, looking at the man keenly.

"I know where she is, the chit yer after."

"Oh, really . . ." Harriet Fordyce scoffed.

"It's true," the man protested. "You'll see it's true. Bill Smith don't lie."

"Produce her," Gerald challenged.

The man looked sly. "Not so fast, fine sir. What's in it for Bill Smith, I'd like to know?"

"I think you must be aware that there's a substantial reward offered for the return of the Ransome heiress," the lawyer told him.

"Yes, I heard tell there's money in it."

"One hundred guineas, if you speak the truth," Mr Pritchett told him, sucking air through his teeth.

"I tell the truth, but I want to be sure I'll not be sent to the beak. A wrong's been done, I'll not deny."

The lawyer glanced at Gerald Fordyce who reluctantly nodded before the man was able to reply, "You have our assurance."

"And I'll get the blunt?"

"If what you say is true but we shall have to be very certain."

"You will be."

"Then first of all tell us how you know her."

"It was me who found her." Harriet Fordyce gasped. "Wanderin' she was, a little mite all alone by the river-bank."

"You abducted her?" the lawyer asked.

"No! It wasn't abduction, not to my mind. Couldn't say 'er name or where she came from. How was I to know who she was? So I took her. What else could I do? If I'd left 'er there she'd 'ave drowned, right enough. 'Ad one little foot

59

in the river when I found 'er, so I know where she was, don't I?"

"Everyone knows where Annabel was when she disappeared," Gerald protested, taking a pinch of snuff.

"You may be sure," the lawyer said severely, "I shall have to be certain it is Annabel before any money is handed over. Now, my good fellow, when may we see this girl?"

"Now. She's outside, sir, awaitin' your pleasure."

Harriet Fordyce gasped again and Mr Pritchett urged, "You had better bring her in with no further delay, Mr. Smith."

The man got up and hurried from the room. Mrs Fordyce stood up and went to her son's side by the fireplace. Mr Pritchett glanced at them. "We must prepare ourselves for a disappointment. I have already received several messages at my chambers which quickly proved useless."

"We don't expect this creature to be poor Annabel," Mrs Fordyce replied. "This tinker must think we're not up to snuff if he attempts to foist this imposter upon us."

Both Harriet Fordyce and her son stiffened as Bill Smith returned dragging by the arm an unwilling girl. Her hair hung loose to her wiast, her old-fashioned gown was in a filthy condition and patched in places. Mr Pritchett made a gesture of distaste as the gypsy propelled the girl into the centre of the room. She stood there looking like a cornered animal.

Harriet Fordyce stared hard at her before crying, "Just look at her hair, Gerald. One thing is evident she is no gypsy."

The girl tossed back the golden mane of hair and rubbed the arm the gypsy had gripped as she looked around her with hate-filled eyes. In a studied gesture Mrs Fordyce looked up to a painting which hung above the mantel. It portrayed a beautiful young woman with dark blue eyes and

60

golden hair, much the same colour as that possessed by the girl. Everyone else followed the direction of her gaze including the lawyer.

"She has Marguerite's hair," Mrs Fordyce gasped. "There's no doubt of that. If only . . ."

"Do not excite your hopes too soon," Mr Pritchett warned and then gently to the girl, "What is your name, child?"

When she didn't answer Bill Smith shook her by the shoulders. "Tell the gentleman."

"Jenna." It was no more than a whisper. "Jenna Smith." She averted her eyes from his searching ones.

"I gave 'er the name," Bill Smith volunteered. "Didn't know—or wouldn't say—'er own. Never spoke of it to this day."

Mr Pritchett cleared his throat. "Well, I own there is a faint resemblance between this girl and the late Mrs Ransome, but we shall need more proof than that, I'm afraid."

"Yes, this is quite absurd," Gerald protested. "You cannot expect us to believe this is my cousin on such flimsy evidence."

"Ever seen a gypsy with such 'air?" Bill Smith asked.

"We are not denying that you may have abducted some poor child," Gerald told him, affecting boredom.

Jenna was looking up at the portrait as Bill Smith eased a locket and chain over his head. "You don't 'ave to take my word for it." Gerald laughed contemptuously. " 'Ad this with 'er, she did. Never 'ad the 'eart to sell it. Don't know why. Got a fondness for the chit. Like my own she's been all these years. Kept a lonely man company."

He handed the locket to Mr Pritchett who opened it whilst a few yards away Harriet Fordyce clung anxiously to her son's arm, before casting a faint smile at Jenna who was

61

now gazing around the elegant salon, appearing to be still bewildered.

The lawyer opened the locket just as Mrs Fordyce came away from her son's side and asked, "What is that?" in a timorous voice.

He held it out for her inspection and she gasped, recoiling slightly. "Have you seen this before, Mrs Fordyce?"

"Not since it was hanging around the neck of my sister-in-law. I remember it well. Those are her initials on the case and the portraits are those of my brother and sister-in-law. Why, I recall now the day he put it around his daughter's neck." Her eyes grew wide as she looked to Jenna again. "Ye Gods!"

She continued to stare at Jenna for a long moment before going to her and enfolding her in her arms. "Welcome home, my dear." Jenna remained unyielding in her arms as Mrs Fordyce whispered in her ear. "You have done splendidly well."

A moment later she drew away smiling at the girl. "Annabel. Our own dear Annabel. We never thought to see you again, my dear. This is indeed a miracle."

Jenna turned on her heel, running to Bill Smith's side. "I'm not Annabel. Don't call me that." She looked at the gypsy. "Don't leave me here. Please don't. I don't want to be their Annabel. I want to be with you, just like before."

He caught hold of her roughly. "Now look 'ere, girl. You do as yer told. See? Yer a fine lady. Yer belong 'ere, not wi'me. If I did wrong in takin' yer, now I'm makin' it right, and if you come after me I'll tan yer hide, Right?"

She continued to look distressed but Mrs Fordyce said soothingly. "Don't fret, my dear. Once we were fond of each other and we welcome you home—where you belong."

"I belong with him," Jenna answered truculently.

"You never did," Bill Smith told her before looking at the lawyer. "Am I to get that blunt?"

"It appears Mr Smith is speaking the truth," Gerald agreed, smiling at Jenna who could not meet his eyes. "This girl is just as I imagined my cousin would be if she were alive, and the locket . . ."

"Why did you not come to my chambers?" Mr Pritchett asked of the gypsy.

The man grinned. "Where's that then? Look, this is where I found 'er and this is where I brought 'er back. Isn't that enough, eh?"

Mr Pritchett answered sighing slightly. "It appears on the face of the matter, this is Annabel Ransome. I shall write a note for you to take to my bank."

The gypsy grinned again. "The blunt is what I want not a piece of useless paper."

"But . . ." the lawyer began to protest.

"I shall give the fellow his money," Gerald offered, coming across the room. "You can repay me at a later date. Mama, why do you not take Jen . . . Annabel to rest for a while? This has been a most terrible ordeal for her."

"What a splendid idea," Mr Pritchett agreed.

As Gerald went out of the room he caught sight of Mrs Tarrand, the housekeeper, hovering in the hall, looking perplexed. "Ah, Mrs Tarrand, good news," he greeted her. "Miss Annabel is come back to her family at last."

The housekeeper's hand went to her lips, and her eyes were wide. "Lord save us!" she gasped. "It cannot be."

"Only look, Mrs Tarrand, and you will see it is so."

Harriet Fondyce led a reluctant Jenna out of the room. "Now, my dear," she said soothingly, "you must rest and bathe, and then we shall find you some suitable clothing."

"Don't want to," Jenna replied sullenly.

"Oh, you will soon grow used to living at the Manor. The

Quality is in your blood and cannot be denied however long you lived with the gypsies."

Mrs Tarrand stared at them, her hand still clapped to her lips. "Is this not splendid to have Miss Annabel back, Mrs Tarrand?" Mrs Fordyce asked of her. The woman just continued to stare. "Is she not the image of her poor dead Mama?"

The housekeeper remained in the hall as Mrs Fordyce led Jenna up the stairs. Halfway up they met Gerald coming down. He paused and grinned at them both.

"Magnificent, Jenna," he whispered as he pretended to kiss her cheek.

"I was so certain I should be denounced," she answered before he drew away.

"You may be certain the old boy is quite persuaded otherwise he would not agree to part with the reward."

He continued down the stairs with a light step but paused in the hall to address the housekeeper again, "Mrs Tarrand, you look as if you have seen a ghost."

"So have we all, Mr Fordyce, but how can anyone be certain it is Miss Annabel?"

"She carries with her proof of her identity. None of us have any serious doubts."

Tears came to the woman's eyes. "Never thought to see the day," she murmured.

"Nor did we," he answered jauntily as she hurried away, a handkerchief held to her lips.

"Mrs Tarrand is quite overcome," he announced when he went into the drawing-room once more. He held up the bag of coins and the gypsy put out a greedy hand to take it from him but Gerald Fordyce did not relinquish the money so easily.

"Just a moment. I trust you will not tarry long around

64

here. It might unsettle Miss Annabel to know you are in the area."

The gypsy laughed. "I'll be off as quick as hell can scorch a feather, sir, you can be certain of that."

"Be sure that you are," the young man told him in a cold voice. "We shall not look to see you around here again."

He dropped the purse into the man's outstretched hand and watched him hurry away. Mr Pritchett moved towards the door. "I am not at all persuaded you should have urged him to leave the area so soon." Gerald looked at him in surprise and the lawyer went on, "I might wish to question him further."

"Are you still in doubt about the girl's identity? If so we should not have paid the rascal."

"I am a lawyer, Mr Fordyce, and I am bound to act in a cautious manner. On the face of it, the evidence is incontrovertible but a lot of money is in question . . ."

Gerald laughed and took out his snuff box. "I know. Half of it would have been mine. Be as cautious as you please, Mr Pritchett."

"Indeed I shall."

The young man inhaled a pinch of snuff. "As to the gypsy, I thought it like the girl might attempt to run off to join him if he remained in the area."

"Quite so. Well, with your permission, sir, I shall remain here a few days longer than originally planned, so I had best go now and pen a note to be sent to London on the morrow."

"Stay as long as you please. This matter must be settled satisfactorily as soon as possible."

"It will be. It would be unthinkable to harbour the girl under this roof a moment longer than necessary if she is proved to be a fraud."

"In truth it is difficult to perceive that stranger as my cousin, but the evidence . . . ."

"This has been a grievous shock to you, Mr Fordyce, but in my heart I am convinced this girl really is your lost cousin."

"We shall see," Gerald answered non-committally, staring past him as if deep in thought.

The lawyer's eyes narrowed. "Do you have serious doubts about the validity of her claim, sir?"

The young man smiled. "Like you, Mr Pritchett, I merely wish to be absolutely certain of it."

As the lawyer walked towards the door he paused to say thoughtfully, "If this chit really is Miss Annabel Ransome you are bound to be a trifle disappointed."

Gerald smiled again. "Indeed. The prospect of even half a fortune was a welcome one, but if my cousin is proved alive and well it is worth the loss of my inheritance."

The lawyer's face broke into a rare smile. "That is a splendid sentiment if I may be allowed to say so, sir."

He turned to the door again as Gerald added, "I cannot, however, guarantee my cousin Hollingdale's delight."

Mr Pritchett nodded and when he had gone the young man walked over to a table which bore several decanters. After a moment's hesitation he lifted one and poured a generous measure of his late uncle's port into a crystal goblet. As he did so he began to laugh. Taking both glass and decanter to the sofa he sat down and, still laughing, he raised the glass to his lips.

SEVEN

Mr Pritchett was just about to go down to breakfast the following morning when he caught sight of Jenna coming out of her room. He was momentarily startled, for although she still appeared to be frightened, her long, undisciplined hair had been pinned into a neat style with wispy curls framing her face and making her blue eyes seem even larger. The grime and dirt had been washed away and she was wearing a black velvet gown which made her appear even younger and more vulnerable than before.

"Good morning, Miss Ransome," he greeted her and she started slightly at the use of that name.

"I shall be obliged to grow accustomed to be called by that name, sir."

He chuckled and then frowned. "You speak well, my dear."

She smiled foolishly. "I was for ever in trouble for mocking my betters. It seems I am doing it now without thinking."

"Can you also read and write?"

"Of course," she retorted, and then bit her lip when he asked, looking surprised, "Who taught you?"

"A curate," she answered breathlessly. "When . . . we camped for the winter he taught us, all those of us who wished to learn."

67

"And where was that?"

Jenna's mind frantically sought out the farthest possible place. "Northumberland," she supplied. "It was somewhere in Northumberland although I cannot say exactly."

He cast her a kindly smile but Jenna was no deceived by it. She must be aware that this man was no one's fool and she must not underestimate his ability. "You must feel very odd indeed at the moment."

"Yes, I do, but I dare say I shall grow used to it. Mrs . . . Aunt Harriet has been very kind although she says I must wear black for a while. Mr Ransome recently died. I cannot in all truth think of him as my father."

"That is very understandable and you must not allow it to tease you, for, if he were still alive, Mr Ransome would find you similarly strange."

Her eyes were wide as she wrung her hands together. "Am I truly Annabel Ransome, Mr Pritchett?"

He frowned slightly. "Do you not feel you are Annabel Ransome?"

Jenna clasped her arms about her as if she were cold. "I . . . don't know."

"It was a foolish question," the lawyer conceded, looking abashed.

"The house is not entirely strange, I feel."

"Excellent. We must discuss it in more detail, but first allow me to take you down to breakfast."

Jenna tossed her head back in a defiant gesture. "First I wish to see the nursery."

"I don't know where that is so shall I ask one of the servants to accompany you?"

"I think I know where it is." One of his eyebrows rose a little and she went on, biting her lip again. "It's just a feeling. There is something definitely familiar about this place. I felt it as soon as I arrived, but everything was too chaotic to realise it at once. Now I know I have been in this house before."

Mrs Fordyce came hurrying along the corridor just then. "Good morning to you both."

She kissed Jenna on her cheek but there was a look of anxiety in her eyes as she drew away. "Did you sleep well, my dear?"

"Not too well, I'm afraid."

"Never mind, dear. You will soon grow accustomed to lying in a feather bed."

She glanced at the lawyer who said, "This young lady declares the house is somewhat familiar to her."

"Indeed." The woman looked intrigued.

Jenna averted her eyes. She was finding deceit and trickery very difficult but knew she had no choice but to continue. That she had been so far successful astounded her.

"Did I sleep in my . . . mother's room last night?" she asked.

"Why yes," the other woman replied. "Did the maid tell you?"

"No one mentioned it. I just knew."

"But you couldn't possible recall that fact."

"Not clearly but I did *know*."

"Lead the way to the nursery, Miss Ransome," Mr Pritchett instructed and held back Mrs Fordyce so that Jenna could go forward on her own.

They followed her along corridors and up a flight of stairs until she reached the nursery at last. Toys still littered the table and little had been changed since the child had left it.

Jenna stood in the doorway, gazing around. "This is remarkable," Mrs Fordyce exclaimed.

"Most nurseries occupy a similar situation in houses of this kind," Mr Pritchett pointed out.

"She couldn't possibly know that, being brought up by the gypsies," the woman responded.

"Quite so," the lawyer murmured.

Suddenly Jenna rushed forward, snatching up a rag doll off the dresser. "Rosie!" she cried. "It's Rosie!"

As she hugged the doll to her Mrs Fordyce said in a choked voice, "That was always her favourite toy. It was found on the river bank the day she disappeared."

Mr Pritchett turned away. "I have no doubt in my mind that this is your missing niece, Mrs Fordyce."

The woman gasped. "It's a miracle."

"I cannot be other than delighted at the outcome, Mrs Fordyce, although I do commiserate with your son and, of course, Major Hollingdale."

"My son is more than delighted to see Annabel back in the family fold again. As for Major Hollingdale, that remains to be seen when—if—he returns to England. If he has any decency about him he too will rejoice."

"May I take Rosie to my room, Aunt?" Jenna asked.

"Of course you may, but do come down to breakfast. I cannot wait to tell Gerald about this, and for him to see you in your gown. We must, of course, have you fitted for more in due course. You must be clothed according to your position."

Jenna laughed. "One gown is enough, surely, Aunt? Especially one as fine as this."

Mrs Fordyce glanced at the lawyer. "Is she not a delight, Mr Pritchett? Such innocence is indeed rare and I pray she will not lose it easily."

"What a pity her father did not live to see her."

Mrs Fordyce looked immediately sorrowful. "Ah yes, it is a great pity, but having her back now is better than never, and seeing her as she is I feel she might never have been away."

She cast a wistful look at Jenna who swallowed and said, "I feel that too—now."

* * *

70

Jenna came away from the drawing-room window as the carriage disappeared around a curve of the drive.

"Thank goodness he has gone. It was becoming unbearable to have him hovering around me all the while."

Mrs Fordyce laughed as she jabbed at her sampler with the needle. "My dear, Mr Pritchett was completely convinced from the moment you snatched up that doll."

"Even so it has been a strain."

"And one you have faced up to splendidly," Gerald told her, gazing at her admiringly across the room. "Even I have to remind myself that you are not Annabel Ransome."

"I thought I would have an attack of the vapours when he asked me if I could read and write, and I answered without a thought."

"You contrived very well," the other woman told her. "You are a natural actress."

Jenna was not amused. "Nevertheless," Gerald mused, "we must watch such matters carefully. Jenna Tregail might well be a lady, but Annabel Ransome cannot be too much of one."

Jenna went to sit on the edge of the sofa. "What happens next?"

"The county will be buzzing with news of your return," Mrs Fordyce told her, "and before long invitations will be arriving, for everyone will be in a fidge to meet you. Then, after a decent interval has passed, your betrothal to Gerald will be announced. It will be a perfect ending to what everyone will look upon as a fairytale."

Jenna's cheeks grew pink at the notion. Gerald Fordyce was both handsome and elegant, but somehow the thought of marriage to him was distasteful.

"What if . . . I am discovered to be a fraud?"

Gerald poured himself a generous glass of wine and laughed. "You have convinced old Pritchett and he is the one who really matters. Everyone else will be easy. The difficult part is over. You can take your ease a little from now on."

"But what if, by some mischance, the real Annabel arrives? I'll wager you had not thought of that."

The young man shrugged his shoulders. "She is dead, I don't doubt, but in the unlikely event . . . she would be turned away as an imposter now you are proved to be she."

He lifted the glass to his lips, laughing as he did so. Jenna eyed him grudgingly. "Nothing would happen to you. You have apparently no connection with me."

"Just continue to act the little Sarah Siddons and all will be well, my dear."

After a moment she asked, "I never really understood what happened to little Annabel."

Mrs Fordyce sighed. "It was a dreadful business. Poor Jack neglected her terribly, mourning Marguerite and leaving the child in the care of nurserymaids. He was never here. He gambled and drank, and could scarce be expected to recognize the child if she were put in front of him.

"One day the nursemaid had an assignation with her lover in the copse by the river. She took the child, ostensibly for a walk, and then while she was enjoying her lover's embrace, Annabel must have grown restless and wandered away. That was the last anyone saw of her."

"How dreadful," Jenna murmured, genuinely moved.

"My brother was distracted, grief-stricken. He offered a fortune for her return—to no avail. As time went on he became more and more unhinged. From being a rake who enjoyed every pleasure he became a recluse, waiting here for Annabel to return until the day he died."

"I always believed he acknowledged her dead until the will was read," Gerald admitted, helping himself to another glass of wine.

"The nursemaid must have suffered terrible guilt too," Jenna commented.

"She was immediately dismissed naturally," Mrs Fordyce told her.

"What became of her? Do you know?"

Gerald put his empty glass down. "They found her that evening, hanging from the stable rafter."

Jenna gasped, her eyes wide. Mrs Fordyce leaned forward to pat her hand. "Do not distress yourself, my dear. It was all a very long time ago."

But Jenna could not easily rid herself of the knowledge so much suffering had resulted from Annabel's disappearance. She couldn't help but wonder how much would arrive with her resurrection.

"Gerald scarce remembers Annabel, but Hollingdale was fond of her, I recall," Harriet Fordyce reminisced.

The young man laughed harshly. "Hollingdale is fond of all females, whatever their age."

Jenna looked at him with interest. "Tell me about this cousin of yours, Mr Fordyce."

"Call me Gerald from now on. We are, after all, supposed to be cousins, and Hollingdale is of no interest to you."

"If he is to be cheated out of his half of the inheritance, I deem him of great interest," Jenna retorted.

"You must be careful what you say," Mrs Fordyce urged in a low voice. "The servants might well be eavesdropping. Most of them do."

"I will remember, but speaking of servants," Jenna went on, "Mrs Tarrand looks at me as if she hates me. 'Tis quite unnerving, for I cannot think why."

"I am persuaded you are being fanciful," the other woman replied in a soothing tone. "The best servants are always aloof."

"Her niece is far more amiable," Jenna pointed out.

"Oh indeed she is," Gerald answered dryly.

"Mrs Tarrand cannot hate you, my dear," Harriet

Fordyce put in quickly, shooting her son a warning look. "However, she has been at the Manor very many years now and no doubt recalls Annabel's disappearance as well as I do. When it happened all the servants were put under a great deal of strain and when the nursemaid. . . . She will grow used to you."

Gerald grinned. "If she does not you can always dismiss her."

The realisation she was the mistress of this great house, albeit as a puppet, made Jenna start. When she understood he was teasing her she retorted, "You know I would not."

"All the same Mrs Tarrand has a fetching neice."

"You mean Grace," Mrs Fordyce broke in.

"She certainly brightens up this sombre place," Gerald told her. "I had no notion she possessed a niece."

"How should we know everything about our servants," his mother admonished. "And allow me to point out, Gerald, that from now onwards you must only have eyes for Annabel."

"That would not normally be easy for me, I own, but with Annabel . . ."

He allowed his words to die away but his look was eloquent enough. Jenna shot him a disgusted glance. "You have not as yet told me anything about your cousin," she insisted after a moment.

"Our cousin," he reminded her, straightening up. "Hollingdale is a rake and a scapegrace. He was for ever in a scrape until my uncle Hollingdale—now deceased and out of his misery—decided his son's dubious talents would be better employed in the fight against Boney."

"You evidently harbour no love for him," Jenna said sarcastically.

"My feelings for Hollingdale are of no account, my dear. However, if he succeeds in evading a Frenchman's shot and does return home, you had best be on your guard, for he is up to snuff and if you make one mistake he will find you out."

She shivered at so dire a warning but Mrs Fordyce said, "You credit him too well and he need not concern Annabel at all."

It seemed odd to be called by such a name, but Jenna knew she must grow accustomed to it. At least allowances would be made for not answering immediately. Everyone knew she had not been known as Annabel for eighteen years.

"I had thought of one thing," Gerald said thoughtfully a moment later, looking at her. "If Annabel lived amongst gypsies she would ride like the wind, would she not?"

Mrs Fordyce shrugged. "No doubt."

"Do you ride, Annabel?" he asked.

At the use of the name her cheeks grew pink. "I ride, but I am sadly out of practice."

"In that case I think I had better give you some lessons." Again she was alarmed and he grinned. "Don't get into a pucker; I shall choose a placid mount until you are able to ride like a gypsy."

Mrs Fordyce put down her sewing and got to her feet. "Gerald has so much good sense. I shall go and find a riding habit for you."

When she had gone Gerald walked across to the window to stare out. Jenna sighed. "To think I only wished to be a companion."

He laughed. "That would have been a sad waste of your talents, my dear. You are quite lovely. I wasn't fully aware of it when we saw you in Newgate but I must declare myself very pleased with my cousin. Most heiresses are bracket-faced and cork-brained to boot. How fortunate it was that I could actually choose you."

She looked away from him in dismay. He was so pleased with himself and yet she almost hated him for forcing her into a charade for which she had no heart.

EIGHT

"You are becoming quite a horsewoman, Annabel," Gerald declared as they cantered into the stable yard.

Jenna patted the horse's neck before she cast him a mischievous look. "And so I should be. Was I not raised with the gypsies?"

"No one would ever doubt it if they see you ride now."

"You are an excellent tutor, I own."

"In many things," he told her, and her cheeks flushed beneath the veil of her riding hat.

To cover an awkward silence he said, "I trust your dancing-master is pleased with you too."

"He declares that he is. I already knew a few steps, but I am far more prepared for when we are out of mourning."

The stableboys took the horses after Gerald had helped her down. "Your attitude seems to have softened towards me of late," he observed as they walked towards the house.

"If we are to be wed then it is necessary we employ some manner of cordiality," she said airily.

"So you don't hate the notion as much as you did?"

"Such an arrangement has its advantages, Gerald. For example, I shall not mind when you chase maid-servants as much as I would if I loved you."

"Are you certain you do not?"

She laughed and as they rounded the corner he stopped to face her, tapping his riding whip against his palm. "Some females have romantic notions for ever in their heads."

She gave him a curious look. "Romantic, Gerald?"

"Let me explain, we shall soon be taking up some of the invitations we have been receiving of late, and you will be meeting a great many people, some of them adoring men. You have become quite a beauty, my dear, but I would hate you to throw your cap over the windmill for one of them."

She began to walk away from him. "I am not so foolish. After all that has happened to me of late I put my trust in no man. Our arrangement will do well enough."

"I am relieved to hear you say so."

"There are advantages for me, apart from the obvious ones. At least I *know* from the outset what a mountebank you are. Such knowledge has its advantages, wouldn't you agree? Your failings will not come as an unpleasant surprise after our marriage."

She began to walk away from him at a brisk pace. "You are unusually bitter," he answered, hurrying to catch up with her again.

"It is a long time since anyone showed me kindness for its own sake, Gerald."

"I have my failings, but I shall not be cruel to you, if that is what you fear."

She smiled without mirth. "No, I'm persuaded you will not, unless I decide I do not want the Ransome inheritance—or you—and then I am sure I will find myself on my way to the Colonies before I am able even to gasp for breath."

"You wouldn't be so foolish." He laughed. "In any event I have it in mind that you like life as the Ransome

77

heiress far too much to think of giving it up on a mere whim."

She gazed at him steadily. "If your deceit ever becomes known to others you may rest assured it will not be on my account." Then she added, looking away from him, "I think it is past the time when I should be changing for dinner."

She brushed past him and he made no attempt to stop her, although his laughter echoed cruelly in her ears as she hurried to her room.

Mrs Tarrand's niece, Grace, had been appointed her maid and as the girl helped to arrange her new mistress's hair, Jenna noted how pretty she was, with colouring only a little darker than her own, and wide blue eyes. Her name was eminently suitable. Jenna didn't wonder that Gerald found the girl entrancing. She certainly bore no resemblance to the dour-faced housekeeper.

"Mrs Fordyce said to tell you some new gowns have arrived from London, ma'm," the girl informed her.

"I am badly in need of them, for I shall soon be out of mourning, and in truth it will be a relief to wear a colour. After all, I am in mourning for a man I never even knew."

"Never knew my father either, ma'am. Died, he did, when I was a babe."

Jenna cast her a sympathetic look. "And I understand your mother also passed on not long ago, Grace."

"Yes, ma'am. Now there's only Auntie . . . I mean Mrs Tarrand. I'm glad I'm settled here."

Grace went to fetch Jenna's shawl before taking the now cold water from the room. Jenna was just about to go down herself when there came a tap at the door. On her command Mrs Tarrand came into the room and Jenna's heart sank for the housekeeper always looked at her so oddly. There were

78

times when Jenna suspected that the women knew her to be an imposter.

"Is everything in order, Miss Annabel?" the housekeeper asked, glancing around the room which Grace had left in perfect order.

"Oh yes, indeed. Is that all you wished to know, Mrs Tarrand?" Jenna was more than anxious for her to leave.

"I have been wondering if there were any changes you wished to make in the running of the household."

It occurred to Jenna then that the fear of this might well be at the root of the woman's apparent hostility. "Why no, Mrs Tarrand. I have no cause to do so. You must run the house as it always has been, and that is quite satisfactory to me, I assure you."

Jenna's words did not seem to please the housekeeper as much as might have been expected. "And Grace, Miss Annabel? Is she suited?"

"Very much so."

"Only she isn't a proper lady's maid. . . ."

"That is of no real account to me. She has to learn, and in truth as you know, Mrs Tarrand, I am not used to having a maid myself. We are both, in fact, learning."

A mirthless smile crossed the woman's face then. "Yes, Miss Annabel, I know that. If you'll excuse me now . . ."

As she went towards the door Jenna said hastily, "Why do you not like me?"

As Mrs Tarrand turned back her face was devoid of all expression. "You are mistaken, Miss Annabel, I can assure you."

Jenna smiled faintly. "I am glad to hear it."

After she had gone Jenna remained uneasy and not convinced that there was any truth in the housekeeper's words. For some reason she did resent her and Jenna wondered if that might be because she preferred to look upon Harriet Fordyce as her mistress. Jenna determined then that she would act more decisively with the servants, although such action would be hard for her to undertake. Servants might appreciate having a firmer mistress, and she knew she must make the effort to appear authoritative however difficult that might prove to be.

A short while after Mrs Tarrand had left she pulled the shawl about her shoulders and opened the door, glancing back wistfully at the room which was once occupied by the much-loved Marguerite Ransome. The knowledge suddenly brought tears to her eyes.

As Jenna walked slowly along the corridor she wondered how well she would be able to uphold the pretence once she was obliged to take up the many invitations which were now arriving at the Manor. As Harriet Fordyce had predicted everyone was in a great fidge to meet her. She would prove to be quite a novelty for a while, much as the animals in the zoo were. At least no one could compare her with a three-year-old child which was one mercy.

Jenna was so deep in thought that she cried out in alarm as the door to one of the unoccupied guest rooms flew open and a tall figure stepped out in front of her.

"I do beg your pardon, ma'am," he said with a bow. "I regret startling you."

Jenna shrank back at the sight of this dark stranger. "Who . . . who are you? What are you doing here?"

He was evidently not taken aback by her appearance for his eyes raked her mercilessly. Although he was a stranger Jenna fancied she had seen him before somewhere and searched her mind.

"Charles Hollingdale at your service, ma'am."

He made another slight bow, but it seemed more in a mocking fashion. He was very elegantly dressed in much the same way as Gerald, but this man was taller and broader, and his dark colouring was an excellent foil for his black hair which curled around his brow and into the nape of his neck.

At the mention of his name she gasped again, staring at him in horror as he regarded her mockingly again. "I doubt if a new housekeeper has been appointed in my absence, so am I to presume that you are my cousin Annabel?"

"They told me you were in the Peninsula," she retorted breathlessly, unable to hide her surprise.

"So I was until I received a letter from my late uncle's lawyer, giving me the joyous news that my cousin had been found—alive and well after all these years. I came home as soon as it could be arranged. The age of miracles certainly isn't past."

Jenna's head swam. Every word was weighted with irony. She forced a smile of welcome to her lips, however, and hoped he could not discern that she was trembling. Gerald's warning about his cousin echoed dismally in her mind.

"We did not look to see you here at this time but be certain I am glad you decided to join us."

He smiled faintly. "Thank you, my dear. How gracious you are. The entire family is now together, something I had despaired of ever seeing again."

Just then Jenna realised why he had seemed familiar to her; he bore a definite resemblance to his uncle—the late John Ransome—whose portrait was prominently displayed in the house and in the locket she was obliged to wear at all times. Charles Hollingdale's eyes strayed to it too.

"Annabel! Annabel!"

Mrs Fordyce's voice filled with anxiety made Jenna turn on her heel, grateful for the interruption. "Here I am, Aunt Harriet."

The woman hurried around the corner and then stopped abruptly when she saw the two together. "So you have

81

already met," she said breathlessly and not with any pleasure.

"Becoming reacquainted," Major Hollingdale corrected, "and most pleasantly surprised by what I perceive. It was a real anxiety that poor Annabel had been transformed into some harridan by circumstances."

As he glanced at her smilingly Jenna felt acutely discomforted. Mrs Fordyce's face relaxed then and she held out her hands to her nephew.

"Charles, my dear boy. Welcome home at last."

He took her hands in his and kissed her cheek. "Aunt Hattie, I declare you look ten years younger than when I last clapped eyes upon you."

"Such moonshine. You could talk Boney out of his aspirations."

"If only that were possible."

He glanced at Jenna who was enjoying the respite from his attention when Mrs Fordyce asked, "Is this not the most wonderful thing, Charles? Annabel is back at Barnston Manor."

He smiled wryly. " 'Tis remarkable, I own. I can scarce wait to hear all about it."

Mrs Fordyce took Jenna's hand in hers and the girl was glad of the support. "Let us go downstairs. Dinner will be served shortly and there is so much to talk about. Gerald will be so delighted to see you. You were always his hero, you know. We both follow the news of the war and be assured we are very proud of you, keeping Boney from the door."

"Not single-handedly, Aunt," he pointed out, glancing at Jenna as they walked towards the stairs.

Harriet Fordyce chattered without pause and Jenna knew it was to help her recover from the shock of Charles Hollingdale's unheralded arrival. "How is dear Daphne?" the woman asked. "Have you seen her since you returned?"

"Yes, I spent a few nights with her. The children have grown incredibly since I last saw them."

There was a momentary pause after which Harriet Fordyce said, "It seems the King is ill again. La! We are like to have the Prince of Wales as Regent. One scarce dare think on it, Charles. No wonder Boney thinks we can easily be defeated."

"He is not finding it such an easy task," the young man assured her.

As they approached the drawing-room Jenna watched him curiously. He was totally at ease, which was remarkable in view of the circumstances. From the look of him it was impossible to tell he had until recently seen the horrors of battle in the Peninsula, nor were there any obvious signs of dissipation in his autocratic features.

Gerald was already ensconced in the drawing room when they walked in through the open doors, looking the relaxed family party. Gerald was nursing a glass of wine and when he caught sight of them he scowled. However, a moment later his face was transformed by a smile of welcome.

"Hollingdale! My dear fellow. Mama told me you had arrived. What a surprise!"

"A welcome one, I trust," his cousin responded in rather a muted tone, glancing up at the portrait of Marguerite Ransome which was hanging over the mantel.

"It couldn't be better. It is only right you are here to see our little Annabel. Tell me, how is the situation on the Peninsula?"

"Horrific," replied Major Hollingdale in a soft voice which nevertheless conveyed his meaning all too graphically.

"But Wellesley is making progress against all those damned Frenchies, is he not?"

"Oh indeed. I'm persuaded we shall win."

83

Gerald put down his glass as Major Hollingdale walked around the room, examining ornaments briefly as if to refresh his memory of them. Gerald walked up to Jenna and put an arm around her waist.

"What do you think of our cousin, Hollingdale?"

"She is enchanting," he replied without looking up. After a moment he did glance at her. "I look forward to renewing our acquaintance at very great length."

Jenna averted her eyes and was hard put not to shudder at what she could only believe was a threat from this man. Mrs Fordyce ventured, glancing nervously at her son, " 'Tis amazing how like poor Marguerite she is."

"Only in coloring," Charles Hollingdale mused. "I cannot perceive any other likeness. In fact, their features are quite dissimilar."

Looking rather vexed Mrs Fordyce persisted, "It has been said she favours me as a girl."

Charles Hollingdale smiled again. "Yes, you were very lovely as I recall, Aunt Hattie. That hasn't changed."

The woman affected a smile and then began to sniff into her handkerchief as she sank down into a chair. "Mama!" Gerald cried in alarm. "What is amiss?"

"Oh, 'tis nothing, dear, just emotion. Happiness in fact. Seeing you all together has long been my dearest wish and now it has come to pass. I am quite, quite overcome."

"Poor Aunt Hattie," Charles said mockingly. "I had never considered you to be so mawkish."

"Oh do try not to be so sarcastic for once, Hollingdale," Gerald remonstrated going to his mother. "Can you not see that Mama is genuinely moved?"

Jenna walked slowly across the room before saying in a thoughtful voice, "We cannot expect Major Hollingdale to be pleased at my return, Aunt. After all, my presence here is a serious financial loss to him."

"And to me," Gerald reminded them, "but I could not be more delighted to have you here."

"You mistake me, Annabel," the other man said quietly. "The return of my cousin is something I have hoped and prayed for since the day she disappeared. We were very fond of each other in those days." He watched her keenly. "I had hoped we might become so again."

Jenna could not meet his steady gaze and she averted her eyes.

"How long do you intend to stay?" Harriet Fordyce asked, dabbing at her eyes with her handkerchief.

"I have no notion. I am on indefinite leave and since a visit has been long overdue I hope to remain here some time, unless Annabel wishes me to go."

Jenna's eyes grew wide. "Oh no . . . Indeed not. I cannot conceive why you should think so. In any event it is not for me to say whether you stay or go."

He smiled. "But it most certainly is, my dear. Have you forgotten you are now the mistress of Barnston Manor?"

Again she was forced to look away. There was a strange feeling in the pit of her stomach every time she was obliged to look at him. She was aware she felt fear but there was something else too, which was even more frightening for she could not recognize it.

After a moment she said, "It would please us all if you were to remain here as long as you wish."

Charles Hollingdale cast her a charming smile. "Such a heartfelt invitation cannot be refused."

For once it was the housekeeper who arrived to announce dinner and the newcomer greeted her warmly. "Tarry! Still running this establishment with your customary excellence I trust."

A smile flitted briefly across her face. "Welcome back, Master Charles . . . Major Hollingdale."

"Thank you, Tarry. It has been too long, but the welcome I have recieved has truly overwhelmed me with its warmth."

"Do you intend to stay for long, sir." The housekeeper looked as uneasy as Jenna felt.

"My cousin has very kindly extended an invitation to stay as long as I wish to remain."

"It will be good to have you back here, sir," the housekeeper told him before turning away.

Charles Hollingdale immediately offered to take his aunt into the dining room. The woman had been looking tense but she bestowed upon him a grateful smile. As Jenna made to follow with Gerald he held her back and she looked up at him, her eyes filled with tears of anxiety.

"Oh Gerald, what are we to do?" she whispered.

"I own his arrival is a misfortune we had not looked for, but do not allow his presence to tease you. It can have no affect upon your situation now."

"But what is he asks questions I cannot answer? He knew Annabel so well as a child."

"It is of no account. You recall nothing of your life here so you cannot answer any questions nor make any error. It is quite simple."

"I do pray you are correct."

"Don't get into a pucker over this. Mama and I are determined to protect you from him at all times."

At the table Jenna was seated facing him, prey to his frequent and disturbing glances. One thing was very much apparent—despite the air of politeness between the two he and Gerald loathed each other, and Jenna had to admit rather reluctantly, although she had always regarded Gerald a fine-looking man, when she saw them together he was the one who faded into insignificance.

NINE

Jenna drew back on the landing when the following morning she caught sight of Charles Hollingdale in conversation in the hall with, of all people, her own maidservant, Grace. He was smiling at her as he spoke and she was blushing to the roots of her hair.

On frequent occasions Jenna had come upon Gerald Fordyce flirting with one or other of the maids, but it had never angered her as did the sight of these two in conversation. They remained unaware of her presence and Jenna noted again how imposing he was, towering over the diminutive maid. This morning he was dressed in a brown riding-coat and buff-coloured breeches. A large diamond pin was tucked into his carefully-folded neckcloth and his Hessian boots were polished to a perfect shine.

After observing them unseen for a few moments she felt she must spare the maid any further moonshine and she began to walk down the stairs towards them. Charles Hollingdale looked up as she came down and he smiled welcomingly, not at all abashed that he had been caught flirting with one of the servant girls.

"Good morning, Cousin Annabel!"

"Good morning, Major Hollingdale."

"Such formality between cousins," he chided. "Did you sleep well?"

"Yes, I thank you." Grace still looked bemused and Jenna said with uncharacteristic sharpness, "Grace, why are you standing there? Do you have no work to do?"

The girl blushed an even deeper hue and, casting Major Hollingdale one last glance, hurried away. He watched her progress across the hall until she was out of sight before turning once again to Jenna who had also been watching the girl.

"What a fetching chit."

"That is something you would be bound to notice," she replied dryly.

"I would have to be blind not to. Mrs Tarrand's niece, I understand. 'Tiz amazing what we do not know about our servants, even though they live with us a lifetime."

"There was no cause for her to give an account of her family history," Jenna replied coldly.

"I do agree, but would it not be pleasant if Mrs Tarrand was discovered to possess several lovely nieces?"

"I really cannot see why, save for the pleasure of Mrs Tarrand in her old age."

He chuckled. "I was allowing my imagination to place them here in service at the Manor. How pleasant it would be."

"For you no doubt. My maid's appearance really has no affect upon me."

He eyed her in amusement. "I can see we shall not easily agree." Then he asked, "Are you taking breakfast?"

"I had mine on a tray in my room, I thank you."

One dark eyebrow rose a fraction. "You are an early riser."

"And I might say the same of you, Major Hollingdale."

"Neither of us should be surprised, for you and I share a common reason for that, I fancy."

Jenna drew in a sharp breath, feeling all the while he was playing some obscure game with her. "And what might that be?"

He was gazing at her steadily. "We are both more used to sleeping under the stars and eating by an open fire."

"I wonder when Aunt Harriet and Cousin Gerald will be down?" she asked in order to change the subject.

He laughed as if aware of her ploy. "Do you not know their habits by now? I'll warrant Cousin Gerald will not be down before noon."

Jenna could not help but smile recalling Gerald's promise. "I'll wager you are wrong, Major Hollingdale."

"You injure me, Annabel. You really do."

His face did indeed bear a look of hurt and she frowned. "It is entirely unintentional, I assure you."

"It is easily remedied. Last evening I noted you addressed my other cousin as Gerald and would wish you to accord me the same distinction. I too have a given name."

"I have known him somewhat longer," she answered.

"I am fully aware of his good fortune in that respect and my stay here is intended to redress the balance."

To Jenna's ears his words echoed with foreboding and then he went on, "We can begin by taking a ride together this morning while Cousin Gerald slumbers."

She drew back, alarmed anew. "Oh no, I cannot."

One dark eyebrow rose slightly again. "I was given to understand you were in the habit of riding each day."

"How quickly you have acquainted yourself with my habits, Major Hollingdale," she told him, unable to conceal the bitterness in her voice.

"There are so many years to span, my dear. I am in a

fidge to achieve it quickly. Why don't you change into your habit while I have the horses brought round?"

Her head went back a little. "And if I do not choose to ride with you?"

"I will be obliged to take it as a personal slight, but I cannot believe you have taken me in dislike after so brief an acquaintance."

Vexedly she turned on her heel, lifting the hem of her gown and began to walk back up the stairs, affecting as much dignity as she could muster. "Ten minutes, shall we say?" he called after her, but she didn't reply.

Still vexed and more than a little worried at the prospect of being alone in the company of this man, Jenna hurried to her room to find Grace there.

"Fetch me my riding-habit," Jenna demanded. When the girl had done so Jenna said, still angry, "In future I would be obliged if you would not waste your time in conversation with the members of the family, Grace."

The girl looked abashed, for Jenna was always so sweet-tempered and easy to please. "Yes, ma'am. I do beg your pardon for this morning, but I didn't know what I should do when Major Hollingdale began to speak to me."

"Never mind about that now. Unhook my gown."

The thought of being alone in Charles Hollingdale's company almost reduced Jenna to panic. Last evening Gerald and his mother had made certain they dominated the conversation and she was only obliged to indulge in general tattle. If they were alone, she thought, he was bound to find her out, although she could not imagine how. If only Gerald could join them. She had never wished for his company so much before.

As Grace hooked up her riding-habit Jenna asked, "Is Mr Fordyce up yet?"

The girl's face grew pink at the very mention of his name.

"Not as far as I'm aware. I believe he rarely rises before noon, ma'am."

"One would think he might today," Jenna muttered and then, putting on her hat and snatching up her gloves, added, "Pray inform him I am gone riding with Major Hollingdale as soon as he rises."

"Yes, ma'am," the girl answered warmly. "It will be my pleasure."

Foolish chit, Jenna thought as she went back down the stairs. Can she not see no happiness waited for her in that direction?

Charles Hollingdale was waiting outside as promised. Two coal-black mares were nearby being held by a groom. Major Hollingdale, who had been pacing to and fro, slapping his riding-whip against his palm, immediately came towards her and beamed a greeting.

"Within the ten minutes. This really is excellent."

Jenna pulled on her gloves. "I have it in mind you are often obliged to await a lady's pleasure."

He laughed. "Whenever I do you may be sure the lady in question is well worth waiting for." Then he added, quite unexpectedly, "I am loathe to say it, Annabel, but black becomes you very well indeed."

Not wishing for compliments from such a practised tongue, she retorted, "I shall be out of mourning by the end of this week."

"Such a short time."

"Aunt Harriet deemed it unnecessary for me to be in mourning for the full year for a man I never knew."

He gazed at her somberly, something as disconcerting as his irony. "That is the saddest thing of all. He would have delighted in you."

Such evident sincerity was too much for her to bear and she walked away, towards one of the horses. Had John

Ransome still been alive she would never have been able to play the part of Annabel. Although Charles Hollingdale was the kind of man who might attempt his own trickery if the chance presented itself she could not help but feel guilty in his presence.

When she was about to mount he waved away the groom and helped her into the saddle before going to his own horse. For a while they cantered sedately, which suited Jenna perfectly but when they reached the fields he urged his horse into a gallop and she was bound to follow suit. He was an excellent rider, even better than Gerald whom she had hitherto admired, but as a comparative novice it was all she could do, not only to keep up with him, but to remain seated. Somehow she suspected he was testing her in some way and Jenna was determined not to fail.

At last he reined in his horse who was breathing heavily and patted its steaming flank. Having acquitted herself reasonably well Jenna allowed herself a sigh of relief.

"Uncle Jack always kept excellent horses," Charles Hollingdale told her. "He had a good eye for cattle."

"He apparently enjoyed everything of the best," Jenna answered guardedly.

He turned to smile at her, apparently unaware that she found his company a heavy strain. "That is a family failing."

She tossed her head back and looked him in the eye for once. "Do you refer to yourself, Major Hollingdale?"

"Myself, Fordyce and Aunt Hattie. You too in time, I dare say."

"Do not be so certain of that."

"I am not," he answered soberly and then asked, "Tell me, Annabel, how do you sleep at night?"

Astonished she gazed at him before stammering, "Very well, I thank you. Why do you ask?"

"Because I do not. You see, for a long time I was obliged to sleep beneath canvas, occasionally without even that. Sleeping in a feather bed is strange to me now, and to you, I should have thought."

At last Jenna realised the trap he had sprung and her mind raced. After what seemed to be an age she answered, "It was strange to me too for a long while but I am used to it now and I sleep excellently. You will as well before long."

"Oh yes, I am convinced of it," he answered with a smile.

He brought his horse to a complete standstill, dismounted and then came round to her. For a long moment he stood there, looking up at her, causing her mouth to grow dry before he asked, "Shall we rest our horses?"

She affected a smile, relieved that there were no more awkward questions. "They deserve it. You ride hard."

"I thought you might prefer it."

"Oh, yes, indeed I do," she assured him quickly.

He handed her down and she was relieved when he relinquished his hold on her quickly, but just for one moment he held her close, gazing into her eyes. It was a most disconcerting experience but then she swiftly turned away, taking the reins and leading her horse on. He led his own and they walked slowly towards the river which marked the boundary of the Ransome estate. They were some distance from the house itself. Since her arrival at the Manor Jenna had discovered the extent of the lands was very great indeed.

"You do not recall me at all, do you?" he asked, and she shook her head. "Of course you were very small and I did not truly expect anything else, but it is such a pity. Small as you were and callow as I might have been, we used to enjoy each other's company a great deal. Why, I often lifted you up before me on my horse which you deemed a great lark.

93

You screamed with laughter the faster I rode. You had the makings of a spirited horsewoman even then."

Tears pricked at the back of her eyes. If only he would stop, she thought, and allow the feelings of guilt to recede for a while.

"Tell me about your return," he urged softly and she did so, recounting the few days she had spent with the gypsies as an account of her entire life.

"Did you regard this Bill Smith as a father?" he asked, his eyes narrowing slightly.

They had paused on the river bank where the horses refreshed themselves in the fast-running water. Jenna stared into its murky depths.

"I knew he was not. He never pretended he was, although he cared for me like a father. With my colouring he could scarce pretend I was a gypsy and I never was truly one of them because of it."

That at least was the truth.

"Were you never curious about your real parents, or where you came from?"

All the while they conversed Jenna kept her head averted, unable to look at him directly. Gerald had always seemed devious but this man, surprisingly, had the look of an honest person, whatever were his morals, and Jenna felt deeply distressed now at being a party to defauding him. It was all very different when he had been only a disdainful name on Gerald Fordyce's lips.

"Bill always said he had found me lost and wandering by a river. He never liked to talk about it, and I was loathe to upset him, but, of course, I did sometimes think of it . . ."

"How did you feel when he told you you were to return home?"

She affected a broken laugh. "I was horrified. I could not see myself in any other life, or with any other people around

94

me, but Aunt Harriet and Cousin Gerald soon made me feel at home, and once I was inside the Manor I felt, in a small measure, a part of it."

He glanced around. "Did you know that this was the spot you went missing?"

She gave a little gasp and was all at once frightened. This was where a child had died and as a result a nursemaid too. The realisation made her shiver.

"No, I didn't know."

"I do beg your pardon if I have shocked you."

"You have no need to apologise. It was something I needed to know."

He was looking at her with a strange intensity. "Were you happy all those years, Annabel?"

The question took her unawares once again. How could she answer? What would Annabel have said? The girl would have been happy knowing no other life than that of a traveller. For herself she realised then, for the first time, she could not remember ever being truly happy. Perhaps she was once when her parents were alive, but that was such a long time ago. She had been content with Aunt Zillah, but never happy. That was something which always evaded her.

"I do not think so," she answered at last, feeling she might just as well be truthful in this matter, if not in many others.

He moved closer to her, making her start. Putting one finger beneath her chin he raised it so that she was forced to look into his face at last. "Are you happy now, Annabel?"

"I . . . I don't know."

"It is, perchance, too soon for me to ask. So much has happened in your life, but you will be happy from now on. Everything will be different; I vow it will."

Once again the lump in her throat threatened to choke her, and it was a relief when he moved away to take hold of

95

the horses again. "Although you have no memory of the past, you still remain a lady," he told her as he handed her up into the saddle again.

"Such things can never be obliterated," she answered. "At least that is what Cousin Gerald says."

"For once he is not wrong," Major Hollingdale replied, smiling oddly. "Breeding is always apparent," he added as he climbed into the saddle.

Much to her relief he began to lead the way back towards the Manor. "Oddly enough," she told him, "I did immediately feel familiar in the house. I knew where the nursery was situated and the name of my favourite doll."

He turned to smile at her again. "Then there is every hope you will one day recall our fledgling friendship."

When they cantered up to the house Gerald was standing on the top step looking furious. He immediately hurried down the steps to help Jenna down from the horse and she was grateful for that.

"It seems I shall have to rise early in future," he observed darkly.

"Please," Jenna begged in heartfelt tones only he could hear as Charles Hollingdale handed his horse back to the care of its groom. "I only wish you had done so this morning."

Straightening up Gerald asked, casting the other man a dark look, "Did you enjoy your ride?"

"With someone as charming as Annabel, how could I not?" Major Hollingdale countered, and then with apparent concern, "I do trust I did not interrupt *your* plans for the morning, but you were still abed when we left."

"There will be other occasions. Annabel and I enjoy our rides together. Do we not, my dear?"

He looked at Jenna who managed to smile and Charles frowned as he said, "I expected to be left far behind but I

96

confess I was surprised by her reticent handling of her horse."

Jenna looked at Gerald in alarm and he laughed uneasily. "You are far too late for that, Hollingdale. I have spent a good deal of time teaching our cousin to ride like a lady."

Jenna drew a small sigh of relief and cast Gerald a rare smile of gratitude. Charles Hollingdale was clever but not quite clever enough.

"I am bound to tell you, you have succeeded admirably," the other man conceded. He smiled affably at the others who continued to regard him with suspicion. As Jenna began to move towards the steps, confident that her ordeal was at last over, he observed, " 'Tis amazing. Your hair has scarce darkened a shade, although it is customary that such fair colouring in childhood does grow darker with time."

She stiffened and Gerald protested. "Our cousin cannot help the colour of her hair no more than you or I, Hollingdale."

Charles smiled at him. "I recall yours was of a similar colour and now it can only be described as dun-coloured."

Gerald's face grew dark and Jenna watched him fearfully. "Is that meant to be an insult, Hollingdale?"

Maddeningly Charles Hollingdale threw back his head and laughed. "My goodness, Fordyce, you are as prickly as a thorn. It was merely an observation and I regret any offence you might have taken."

Gerald Fordyce looked a mite foolish then but his anger remained. "You would do well to keep your observations to yourself in the future."

"As you wish, Cousin."

Still looking amused Charles Hollingdale hurried up the steps and Gerald said in low harsh tones, "He is insufferable. Always was and always will be. One of these days I'll curry his hide."

97

"He makes me feel afraid. He seems so suspicious."

He gave her a searching look. "What has he been saying? Or asking?"

"Nothing I couldn't answer adequately on this occasion, but even so, I *am* afraid."

The young man's eyes burned darkly. "Perchance it is time we began to display our fondness for one another. Once we are leg-shackled he can go back to his regiment, or better still to the Devil. Casualties are high out there, but even if he does return he will no longer be welcome in my house."

Jenna would have stepped back if Gerald had not caught her with his hand about her waist. With one glove hand he turned her face to his.

"He has just paused to glance back at us. So much the better. Look as if you adore me, Annabel, dear. You have managed to convince everyone that you are a lady, so this should not require so great an acting ability."

"We have agreed to wed; is that not enough for you?"

He laughed and it must have appeared to be a very intimate scene viewed from the top-most step where Charles Hollingdale had paused. With a determined effort Jenna pulled away from his unwelcome embrace, gasping, "You're hurting me, Gerald."

"You will have to do better than that, my dear," he sneered and she shivered. "Do not be in any haste to forget from where you are come and to where you may yet go."

The threat hung in the air between them for a moment before he released her and turned on his heel, marching up the steps. As she watched him go her eyes misted with tears of frustration and fear. Jenna could not help recall she had experienced no such revulsion when Charles Hollingdale had held her briefly close to him a short while earlier.

TEN

The door opened only slightly, causing Jenna to start a little. She was sitting on the window-seat of the library, gazing out across a wide expanse of lawn which gave way in the distance to patchwork fields. The library was where she often sought, and found, sanctuary when she wished to be alone.

"Ah, so this is where you are hiding." The door closed behind Charles Hollingdale as he came further into the room. As he did so she fought back the alarm which always assailed her when he approached. "Fordyce was seeking you everywhere a little while ago. Evidently he did not look in here."

"I will go to him now."

Jenna began to get up and he went on, "Don't trouble, Annabel. It's too late. He has gone out alone, a disappointed man."

He glanced around at the high bookshelves crammed with leatherbound volumes. "Do you often retreat in here?"

"If I admit to it you will know where to find me in the future."

He laughed, not at all put out by her cool welcome. He sat down a respectable distance from Jenna on the window-seat and spread his arm along the ledge towards her. His proximity was, however, rather discomforting, she found.

"It is understandable that you wish to be alone at times to ponder on your vastly changed fortunes." She laughed harshly, for he could not imagine how much they had changed.

He hesitated a moment before asking, "Do you miss Bill Smith, the gypsy?"

"No," she answered truthfully. "I cannot admit that I do—at least not any longer."

His gaze was an unfaltering one. "That is a blessing." He looked around. "Your father spent a great deal of his time in this library with his books after you disappeared."

"Before that he was always in London, I believe."

"He sought forgetfulness in the usual manner, but I don't believe he ever found it. Afterwards . . . he changed utterly after your disappearance."

Jenna didn't really want to hear about John Ransome, for such references inevitably racked her with guilt, and she murmured, "I know."

He leaned forward slightly. "Once you are properly settled, you will be urged to find a husband. . . ." She looked up in alarm to see that he was not smiling. "Annabel, you must not allow anyone to hurry you. It is too important a choice."

"Who is like to do so?" she asked resentfully, although she knew full well he referred to Gerald.

"The gentlemen who would wish to marry you."

"I cannot possibly think about such matters. I am not yet accustomed to being Annabel Ransome." She got to her feet at last. "Pray excuse me, Major Hollingdale; I have some matters which needs must be attended to without delay."

He stood up too and she was aware he was watching her

as she walked out of the library. Outside she paused to draw in a deep breath, wondering why he had such a disconcerting affect upon her at all times. It wasn't as if she disliked him. For some reason, despite his being a threat to her, she could not.

Afraid he might follow her out of the library she hurried up the stairs to encounter Mrs Tarrand coming out of her bedchamber. The woman looked alarmed as Jenna asked, "Were you looking for me, Mrs Tarrand?"

"No, ma'am. I . . . I was merely checking the linen."

She bobbed a little curtsey and hurried away, watched by Jenna who, a moment later, hurried into the room and thankfully closed the door behind her.

"What a difference wearing a colour makes," Grace observed, touching Jenna's blue satin evening gown with due reverence.

"I own it is good to be out of mourning."

"That's no wonder. In the circumstances I expect you felt it foolish to be wearing black."

Jenna cast her a sharp look. "What makes you say so? What circumstances do you mean, Grace?"

"Seemed silly for you to wear black at all, ma'am. You didn't know Mr Ransome, so how can you mourn him?"

Jenna relaxed a little. "That is true. How odd it must seem to outsiders. Did you know him, Grace?"

"Not very well. I didn't come here until after Mr Ransome had taken badly, but Aunt . . . Mrs Tarrand says he was a handsome man in his youth even though he did lose his reason after you went, not that he seemed to care much before. Never bothered with you at all, Mrs Tarrand says. Ignored you and acted as if you weren't here. Not that he was at the Manor very often, not until after . . ."

"Now, now, Grace stop this gossiping and get Miss

101

Annabel ready for the evening. You were not engaged to gossip."

The housekeeper had come into the room unseen and Grace jumped at the scolding. "Take away the water now," Mrs Tarrand ordered. "I shall fasten Miss Annabel into her gown."

Jenna had no time to wonder why the housekeeper had come into the room; her mind was firmly fixed on the evening to come and the ordeal it presented.

"My nerves are quite overset at the prospect of attending Lady Fairfax's rout," Jenna confided as Mrs Tarrand began to fasten the gown. "I am told the entire county is like to be there too."

"Have you never attened a rout before, Miss Annabel?" Jenna laughed. "How could I?"

Mrs Tarrand paused before she said, "Lady Fairfax is a fine lady, for all she's top-lofty. No doubt you'll find everyone attentive to you and anxious to converse."

"Even if I had attended a dozen routs that would be why I felt alarmed."

"Oh no doubt you will discover it a pleasant experience."

It was rare for Mrs Tarrand to be so garrulous. Normally she did little but stare at Jenna malevolently and spoke only when addressed first. When she had finished fastening the gown Jenna looked at her curiously.

"You remember me as a child, don't you?" Jenna's tongue almost stuck when she said "me".

The housekeeper smiled without mirth as she began to tidy the room, putting away Jenna's discarded clothing. "Bless you, yes. Very fond of Miss Annabel I was."

"You must have been quite overset by the disappearance."

She hesitated for a moment, looking into space, her mind far away. "So were we all, ma'am."

"The nursemaid's death was a terrible thing. Did you know her?"

Mrs Tarrand seemed to stiffen before she answered, "It was her own fault."

"It was a harsh punishment, nevertheless."

"She was entrusted with the child and she failed in her duty, ma'am. She was engaged for nothing else but to care for Miss Annabel."

Changing the subject Jenna said in a thoughtful voice, "You must have known Major Hollingdale in those days too."

The nearest thing to a smile crossed the woman's face. "Yes, I knew Master Charles very well also. His mother ailed, you see, and he spent a good deal of his time here with Miss Annabel, which was odd, for he was a wild boy. Quite un-disciplined at times—I cannot tell you the number of wicked things he did to torment the servants—but for all that he has grown into a fine gentleman."

Jenna put her head to one side a little. "Mrs Tarrand, why do you never refer to me directly?"

"Don't know what you mean, ma'am," she replied putting Jenna's black gown carefully into the press.

"You always refer to Miss Annabel as if she were a different person."

The housekeeper's cheeks grew red and it was the first time Jenna had seen her exhibit any emotion since that first evening when she appeared understandably shocked by Jenna's appearance.

"I do beg your pardon, ma'am. I trust I did not offend you."

"It does not offend me; it is merely perplexing."

For a moment the woman seemed at a loss for words and

then she answered haltingly. "It's just that you take some getting used to after all these years when you were considered dead. I still think of Miss Annabel as a child."

"I understand," Jenna told her, but in truth she did not.

Although Jenna knew she was not Annabel Ransome, Mrs Tarrand could not possibly share the knowledge. The housekeeper handed her a reticule and cloak and with no further word spoken between them Jenna went down to join the others who awaited her in the drawing-room.

Harriet Fordyce was still wearing black and Jenna could not now imagine her in any other colour. "You look quite, quite splendid," the woman said gleefully when she caught sight of her hovering in the doorway.

Jenna smiled faintly, feeling self-conscious. "Thank you, Aunt Harriet. I hope I'm not too late."

"We were wondering where you might be," Gerald told her.

"I was conversing with Mrs Tarrand."

"About what . . . ?" Gerald asked suspiciously.

'Nothing of any account,' Jenna replied, casting him a cool look.

"Is it any of your concern?" Major Hollingdale asked, affecting a slightly surprised air as he came into the room after Jenna.

"Good evening, Charles," his aunt said quickly to forestall any argument. "We were just thinking that Annabel will be sure to eclipse every other female present tonight."

"Without a doubt," Gerald gallantly agreed, although he still looked somewhat annoyed.

Both men were wearing evening-dress, although Charles Hollingdale looked the more handsome. It was as if Gerald studied his elegance too much, while the other man achieved a better effect without ever seeming to try.

104

Slyly Gerald asked, "Do you not agree, Hollingdale?"

His cousin seated himself in a high-back chair and answered languidly, "Cousin Annabel does indeed look fetching but as to her outshining all others . . ." his eyes lingered upon her momentarily but it was long enough to make her cheeks burn. "I shall let you know better when I have inspected the other females at the Fairfax's."

"Such a funster," Mrs Fordyce laughed, although the strain of her nephew's stay showed plainly on her face. "You are forever setting the table in a roar."

"I hope my cousin finds a female to his liking at the rout," Gerald said, "for it will mean I can have Annabel's company to myself."

"I thought you already had," the other man remarked, not troubling to hide his sarcasm.

"I am delighted to admit we have a natural affinity," Gerald protested. "Is that not so, my dear?"

He looked across the room at Jenna who, in truth, was smarting at Charles Hollingdale's deliberate snub. However, she affected a smile which she directed towards the younger man. "So it would seem."

"Success at last," observed Charles Hollingdale dryly as he got to his feet, dominating the room with his presence. "If I recall correctly the Fairfax's had a daughter . . ."

"Several," his aunt supplied, "and only one wed. No doubt they are hoping tonight's rout will remedy that."

"It probably will," Charles replied in a careless tone. "If I recall they were all fetching chits, even in the nursery."

Mrs Fordyce laughed. "You are incorrigible, Charles, and I am persuaded you will find the Fairfax girls very much to your taste."

"Thank you, Aunt," he replied.

Ignoring his heavy irony she added, "Naturally, I am in a fidge to see you respectably settled. It is not before time."

"And I thought you were fond of me," he retorted, eyeing her in amusement.

"There are worse fates," Gerald told him, glancing meaningfully at Jenna.

"I cannot think of many," his cousin retorted, smiling wryly.

As the clock struck the hour Mrs Fordyce said, with evident relief, "It is time to leave."

Charles Hollingdale came across the room and took Jenna's cloak, looking into her eyes, he said, "Allow me, Annabel."

She was glad enough to turn her back on him as he put the cape around her shoulders. For a moment she felt the touch of his fingers on her neck and she shivered although it was far from cold.

"There, let us be gone," he said, stepping back at last.

Harriet Fordyce monopolised his attention and as always Gerald fell into step at Jenna's side. Since her one lone ride with Charles Hollingdale, Gerald had been as good as his word. He had not allowed her to be alone with his cousin on one occasion since.

"I think we have underestimated Hollingdale's disappointment in the loss of the inheritance," Gerald told her in a harsh whisper as they walked to the waiting carriage.

Jenna looked up at him in alarm. "Why do you say so?"

"I know him. This facade of heedlessness hides something quite different, I'm certain."

"What do you think he will do?"

"Nothing, but we must remain on our guard."

"I cannot conceive why you should think it is so, Gerald."

He smiled grimly as he stared ahead at his cousin in amicable conversation with Mrs Fordyce. "Hollingdale was here when the child disappeared."

Jenna looked bewildered. "What has that to do with anything?"

He looked at her for a long moment before asking, "Who knows what part he might have played?"

Charles Hollingdale was at that moment handing his aunt into the carriage. Jenna stopped in her tracks to look at Gerald. "You cannot possibly mean that."

"Why not?"

"He adored Annabel. He told me so."

Gerald's lips twisted into a travesty of a smile. "*He* told you so. Don't be so naive, my dear. What else should he tell you?"

Jenna was on the defensive. "Why should he want to do such a hideous thing?"

Gerald shrugged. "I cannot say. Mayhap he wished to become my uncle's heir. I cannot say what the machinations of his devious mind may be."

Jenna's eyes opened wide in horror. "Gerald, if that is true he must *know* I am not Annabel.

The young man grinned and it was not a pleasant sight. "But he can do absolutely nothing about it."

Charles Hollingdale was awaiting them by the carriage. Jenna glanced at him and he looked at her expectantly. Suddenly she shivered, for quite a different reason this time.

"Come along, you two," Mrs Fordyce called. "It would not do to be late for the Fairfax's."

They began to walk towards the carriage, Gerald looking devilishy pleased with himself, but Jenna's mind was full only of dark thoughts.

ELEVEN

To Jenna's surprise Fairfax Hall was, when they approached, even larger and grander than Barnston Manor, something she would never have believed until then.

A great many guests were arriving for the rout at the same time their carriage bowled up the drive, and it seemed to Jenna all her worst fears were to be realised; half the county would be there.

"Do you dance?" Charles Hollingdale whispered as they waited their turn to be presented to Lord and Lady Fairfax and their family, three girls, all of whom were indeed handsome. Irrationally Jenna disliked them on sight.

"Aunt Harriet engaged a dancing-master for me, so I do know the steps even if I am not very accomplished as yet."

"You must be being modest." He looked at her curiously. "Our mutual aunt has been very accommodating considering you have displaced her son as heir to the fortune."

"And you, Major Hollingdale. Do not forget you have lost as much as Gerald."

"It is not quite the same, for I never expected to inherit a penny."

Feeling bound to defend Mrs Fordyce, Jenna added,

"Both Aunt Harriet and cousin Gerald could not have been kinder to me."

"So I have observed. 'Tis amazing." Before Jenna had any opportunity to think up a stinging rebuke, he said, "Save the first country dance for me, Annabel."

Taken aback she retorted, "Will you not be too busy with the delightful Misses Fairfax?"

He chuckled. "Not during the first country dance if you agree to save it for me, and have no fear I shall find time for all of you this evening."

Vexed, she turned away as, on her other aside, Gerald reflected in a whisper, "The Fairfax girls are indeed fetching chits. Hollingdale was always a menace with females. It is really unfair of us to thrust him in the midst of these unsuspecting creatures. You are more than fortunate I am here to protect you from his taradiddle."

Jenna could not help but laugh and whispered in reply, "Gerald, if you were not here, neither would I." He looked startled and she said, "I do believe you have come to regard me as Annabel Ransome."

"Indeed I do. If you are never to betray yourself you must think so too."

The thought of living her life in the guise of another was daunting although the alternative was even more unthinkable.

When they reached the head of the curving staircase they were duly presented to Lord Fairfax and his wife who declared her delight at Annabel's return and promised a coze on the subject at a more convenient moment. Watching Charles Hollingdale kiss the hands of the young Fairfax girls and the effect upon them as they blushed and giggled, Jenna could readily understand their feelings. Undeniably he possessed a clever way with women, be they old or young, and everything about his manner proclaimed him sincere.

The ballroom was already crowded when they walked in. Before them was a scene of myriad colours. The thought that it was like a gathering of peacocks passed through Jenna's mind. Mrs Fordyce stayed close, something for which Jenna was grateful, for every person in the room was a stranger to her although most of them wished to become acquainted.

So large a gathering could not help but be an ordeal for her, being so unused to the social niceties. Aunt Zillah's card parties for local worthies was the most prestigious she had attended up until then.

As soon as they reached the ballroom Gerald went immediately to avail himself of some of the plentiful champagne, and Charles Hollingdale drifted away into the crowd although Jenna frequently caught sight of him amidst a host of people, mostly females she observed, and all of them hanging on to his every word.

Jenna herself did not have time to feel out of place, for so many people were anxious to speak with her. Most of them declared they had known her as a child and were avid for details of her gypsy life. Travelling towards Barnston Manor with Bill Smith and his band she had learned a little of their way of life and was able to answer all questions satisfactorily. Any awkward moments were bridged by Harriet Fordyce who remained doggedly at her side.

When the country dance was announced Jenna stiffened and sure enough Charles Hollingdale emerged from the crowd and came towards her. Looking at him as dispassionately as she could, Jenna couldn't truly believe he had had any hand in a child's disappearance, and yet she knew so little about him. If Gerald Fordyce was a villain, his cousin could be an even greater one.

He glanced over her shoulder which made her frown. "What is it? Is there someone you know over there?"

He cast her a smile. "I was looking for our cousin. He is rarely to be found far from your side nowadays."

She felt vexed again. His sarcasm always held a ring of truth. "I am greatly attached to my cousin," she declared although it pained her to do so.

"And he to you, 'tis evident, but not just now. Mayhap tonight the champagne is the greater attraction. He was always a trifle cork-brained."

"Am I supposed to be flattered by such a statement, Major Hollingdale?"

"Not if you don't wish to be," he replied with maddening aplomb. "Let us take to the floor with no further delay, Cousin, before anyone else snatches you away."

As they waited in the set Jenna eyed him curiously and she wondered what really was behind the charming exterior. "You really are the most unlikely soldier," she observed.

"I am in agreement with you on that score. I have to confess it was not my idea to join the army. My father, who then controlled the purse strings, insisted I join his old regiment in the hope I would mend my scapegrace ways."

"And did you?" she challenged.

He smiled. "There are those who would say I did not, but I did find I liked the life fighting for my country as opposed to squabbling over some unworthy female."

She looked surprised. "I believed you to be an ardent admirer of females and a champion of their cause."

"So I am. Moreover, the lack of female companionship in the Peninsula had increased my admiration tenfold. I am more aware of their beauty and charm than I ever was before."

Jenna could not help but laugh. The problems which plagued her seemed far away just then. "Gerald was quite persuaded you would have your fill of female company in Spain."

"I wonder what makes our cousin so knowledgeable about life in the army."

"Mayhap his knowledge is confined to his understanding of you."

"It must be, for Cousin Gerald can have no notion of what conditions are like over there. It can be disconcerting trying to make love with the cries of the injured and dying all around."

His words were light but his eyes were full of pain and Jenna was immediately sorry for being so trite. "Was it very terrible?"

"Hell on earth at times. You couldn't possibly imagine."

Her own eyes clouded at the memory of Newgate. "Do not be so certain."

There was a question on his lips but the musicians struck up a tune and the dance began before he could ask it. After that there was little opportunity for conversation but as their hands met and parted in the set she was able to reflect how drastically her fortunes had changed since leaving Penzance. That naive girl who boarded the London coach had gone for ever. Jenna felt she had reached the very lowest ebb humanly possible, only to be elevated beyond expectations to the cream of Kentish Society. The future was one thing she dare not contemplate, but she supposed that marriage to Gerald Fordyce a small price to pay for wealth and position, and, more important, safety. In the past few months Jenna had come to enjoy the position she held, but she still could not understand why her heart was suddenly so heavy.

When the dance ended Charles Hollingdale bowed. "You dance very well indeed, Annabel."

"Are you surprised?"

"I shouldn't be. You excel at so many things. One can almost imagine you were never away from the world into which you were born."

She looked amused. "Do you think I would be better used dancing barefoot around a camp-fire?"

He laughed. "Did you ever do such a thing, Annabel?"

She smiled, refusing to be riled by him. "You have a romantic notion of gypsy life, Major Hollingdale."

"You must acquaint me with the truth of the matter."

His eyes held hers and it was a great effort for her to look away. When she did it was to see Gerald, glaring at them from the doorway. She returned a defiant look. If he wanted to keep her to himself he should have remained at her side. However, she was glad he had not, for her dance with Charles Hollingdale had been more enjoyable than she had imagined. Moreover, his constant badinage was most stimulating.

One of the Fairfax girls came up to them, saying breathlessly, "Oh, Miss Ransome, how delighted I am to make your acquaintance."

"And I yours, Miss Fairfax."

The girl's eyes were wide. "I can scarce credit what happened to you. It is like one of Mrs Radclyffe's gothic novels. Do you not agree, Major Hollingdale?"

He smiled wryly as he stroked his cheek. "I cannot confess to having read any of them. Perchance I should remedy that omission at the first opportunity."

The girl chuckled. "I am addicted to them. Mama says I shall ruin my eyesight. And you, Miss Ransome, do you read gothic novels?"

Jenna was just about to agree when she became hesitant and said instead, "Books have not, until now, been readily available to me, but I shall certainly find time in the future. I have heard said Lord Byron's poetry is well-worth the read."

"Oh indeed, Miss Ransome. You must not be allowed to miss such pleasures a moment longer. Allow me to send some over to the Manor."

Jenna's cheeks grew pink, for in Penzance she had been a frequent visitor to the circulating library and had read every novel and volume of poetry almost as soon as it was published. "That is very kind of you, Miss Fairfax, but I couldn't possibly allow you. . . ."

"Nonsense. It will be a pleasure to have an excuse to call upon you." Involuntarily her gaze strayed to Charles Hollingdale who said, "I would venture to point out no writer of novels, however proficient, could invent such a story as that which happened to my cousin."

"No, indeed," Miss Fairfax agreed. "No one can talk of anything else at present. How romantic it is. I am longing to hear all about it from your own lips, Miss Ransome."

Charles Hollingdale was staring past them and cried, "Ah, Fordyce, there you are. We were wondering what had become of you."

Gerald was approaching them with rather an uneven gait and Jenna realised he was already foxed. "Annabel's going into supper with me, Hollingdale," he announced, a trifle belligerently.

"I am delighted to hear it," his cousin responded. "I am engaged to escort Miss Fairfax. We are both the most fortunate of men."

The girl dimpled and was evidently happy to walk away in his company, but not before she said to Jenna, "I shall call in with a selection of novels at the earliest opportunity."

Jenna watched them go rather wistfully and then when she looked at Gerald she grew angry. "You presume too much, Gerald. You had not asked me into supper and I certainly haven't agreed."

His eyes narrowed when he looked down upon her. "Don't become missish with me, madam. Recall who you are."

"You will never allow me to forget it."

"Once we are wed you may forget. In the meantime I shall escort you into the supper room and then we shall dance together for the rest of the evening. That should prepare everyone for the announcement to come."

"How flattering. It would seem I am a greater attraction than the champagne, but however shall you contrive to stand up for the dances, Gerald?"

"Be certain that I shall." He began to escort her through the crowds. "And do not flatter yourself Hollingdale is smitten with your charms, my dear. He will not have given up on trying to catch you out, you may be sure." The knowledge, which she didn't deny was true, both saddened and depressed her. Gerald's hold tightened on her arm. "Is there any sign that my cousin suspects you?"

"How can I tell?" she asked, suddenly bitter. "His thoughts are never apparent."

The young man chuckled. "Whatever his thoughts or his knowledge might be it is certain he is powerless to act."

Jenna saw him in the supper room the moment they entered, standing head and shoulders above all the other men present. Susannah Fairfax was gazing up at him raptly as he conversed with her in his customary charming way.

"I am helpless too," Jenna thought despairingly, caught as surely as a fly in a pot of honey.

TWELVE

Jenna was at the far end of the formal garden when she heard footsteps approaching along the path. She looked up, always alarmed when approached, for she feared to see either Gerald or his cousin, for different reasons. However, it was one of the footmen who approached, bowing slightly before her.

"Mrs Fordyce sent me to inform you that Lady Fairfax has called and your presence is requested in the drawing-room, ma'am."

Jenna sighed almost imperceptibly as she closed the book she had been reading. "Very well. Tell them I shall be there presently."

As the lackey went back towards the house to do her bidding she watched him go, feeling unequal to meeting Lady Fairfax again, knowing there would be searching questions to answer. However, a few minutes later she put up her parasol and walked slowly back towards the house too. She paused outside the drawing-room to remove her bonnet and to tidy her hair, before taking a deep breath and nodding to the footman who threw open the door.

Lady Fairfax looked no less imposing than she had at her own rout. She was seated on a sofa chattering to Harriet

Fordyce while Susannah Fairfax sat a little further away, looking bored and restless. The conversation had stopped when Jenna entered, bobbing a curtsey to their elevated visitor. Immediately Miss Fairfax's countenance brightened although Jenna had the feeling the girl wished see someone else enter the room.

"Ah, so here you are!" Mrs Fordyce cried. "Only see who has honoured us with a visit."

Jenna affected a smile of welcome too. "I'm so sorry to have kept you waiting, Lady Fairfax. I came as soon as I heard of your arrival."

"How pleasant it is to see you again," the woman declared, eyeing her critically.

"Your rout was so enjoyable," Jenna told her. "It was my very first, you see."

As the woman continued to eye her curiously, Jenna cast an appealing look at Mrs Fordyce. "What an honour that is for us," Lady Fairfax responded with a little laugh. "Tell me, how are you adapting to your new life, my dear? From all I perceive I should say very well."

Jenna looked suitably abashed at the praise. "You are so kind to say so, ma'am, but I own Aunt Harriet has been an invaluable help. Without her guidance I regret to say I should not have been anyone you were like to want in your house."

"You are uncommonly candid."

"I hope I do not offend with my honesty."

Lady Fairfax laughed again. "Indeed not. It is very refreshing."

"We were obliged to teach her all manner of things," Harriet Fordyce confided. "Happily Annabel learns quickly. However, there were times when she found living inside a house quite difficult. The poor child was for ever yearning to be outdoors. Indeed she still does."

"Aunt Harriet is correct. I was in the garden when news of your arrival reached me."

Hopeful that the questioning was ended Jenna gravitated towards the young girl who looked avid for conversation. Susannah Fairfax reached out for a pile of books as the two young ladies sat down together on a sofa. The two older women began conversing between themselves once again much to Jenna's relief.

"I brought these for you, Miss Ransome, as promised. I hope you will find them of as much interest as I did."

"How kind of you to remember," Jenna responded, noting that she had read all of them. "I can scarce wait to begin reading them."

"When you have done so, we must have a coze on their content."

Jenna smiled faintly. "I shall look forward to that."

After a moment the girl began to look rather coy and said, "How fortunate you are, Miss Ransome."

Jenna cast her a questioning look. "Because I am come home?"

"Yes, indeed, but not solely on that score. You have two very handsome cousins living here at the Manor."

The statement caused Jenna some amusement. "I had not considered that a cause for envy, but I dare say it is so."

"There are few of us at the rout who did not envy you their attentions."

"I believe they feel . . . protective towards me in view of my past."

"Oh, more than that, surely. They evidently have a keen regard for you." She paused before venturing as she plucked at her reticule, "The tattle is that you and one of your cousins will make a match before too long a time has passed."

Jenna laughed uneasily. "I cannot think what has given rise to such speculation, Miss Fairfax."

"Oh, Miss Ransome, you can confide in me. I swear I shall not utter a word of what you tell me. Do you favour one of your cousins? I am in a fidge to know the truth of the matter. 'Tis all so romantic!"

In view of the fact one day soon a betrothal would be announced Jenna could see no point in prevaricating any longer, however painful it was to admit it, and she replied in a low voice, "Yes, yes, I do. Mr Fordyce is very much to my taste and I to his."

The girl clapped her hands together gleefully. "How famous! Of course I knew it. He is so handsome. I could not be more pleased for you, and in exchange for your confidence I may tell you Major Hollingdale is very much to *my* taste."

Alarmed, Jenna looked at her as the girl went on, not trying to hide her excitement, "I knew it could not be Major Hollingdale who was about to come up to scratch because of the attention he bestowed upon me. You must have noted it at the rout."

Indeed, Jenna had, much to her chagrin. Charles Hollingdale had fairly danced attendance on the girl while Gerald momopolised her after that one country dance. All the while Gerald was becoming more and more foxed. At the end of the evening it was Charles who was obliged to help his cousin into the carriage, the man she would be obliged to marry before long. How Charles would despise her for that.

"He called in at the Hall yesterday," Susannah Fairfax was saying and Jenna returned her attention to the conversation, "to take us riding, and he really made no secret of his regard for me. My sisters were most envious."

For some reason the girls' words sent Jenna's spirits plummeting. "I had no notion," she murmured.

"It is very soon as yet to say *anything*, but I live in hope. In any event Major Hollingdale is exceeding good company."

As if aware of the conversation the door opened and this time Charles Hollingdale himself came into the room. Susannah Fairfax's cheeks grew rosy at the sight of him, her eyes bright. There was, however, no such enthusiasm on his face, for any of them. There was no way of gauging how he felt about the girl although Jenna realised it was none of her concern.

"Ah, Charles," his aunt greeted him. " 'Tis good of you to join us."

"How could I resist once I learned no less than four fetching ladies were ensconced in the drawing-room?"

Even Lady Fairfax began to simper at his flummery. As he raised her hand to his lips she said, "We are all gratified to see you home safely from the Peninsula, Major Hollingdale."

"It is a relief to me too," he answered in his customary flippant manner.

"You must have been present when Sir John Moore was killed at Corunna. What a dreadful business that was."

"Yes, ma'am. It was a grievous blow to our forces and to me personally."

"On a happier note, my daughter is in a fidge to meet you again," the woman said, glancing across the room at her.

Susannah Fairfax was indeed looking at him hopefully as he replied, "If only I were an artist, so I many capture the vision of two such fetching females."

A moment later he did approach them, glancing briefly at Jenna who began to examine the books in detail. "What a pleasure this is, Miss Fairfax, and so soon after our last meeting."

"My sisters have charged me to tell you how much they enjoyed our ride."

"No more than I, I assure you, and I am pleased to see you enjoying my cousin's company. Mayhap, on the next occasion, I shall bring her along too."

The girl looked less than enthusiastic at the prospect but she smiled nonetheless. "It is a great pleasure becoming acquainted with Miss Ransome. I feel we shall become great friends."

Major Hollingdale looked at Jenna keenly. "It pleases me to hear you say so, for my cousin has few friends outside the family."

'How odd that seems to me," the girl replied. "Miss Ransome, you must look upon me from now onwards as your bosom friend. There shall be no secrets between us."

Charles Hollingdale sat down in a chair close by them and sat back, looking rather pleased with himself. Jenna could only feel a good deal of foreboding although she wasn't sure whether it was because of Susannah's friendship or her budding association with this maddening, enigmatic man.

"Do you harbour any amibitions, Grace?" Jenna asked her one morning as the maid tidied the room.

Looking at her as she worked Jenna realised that if the girl had been born into an elevated family she would have been considered quite a beauty. Now, doomed to servitude, she could only hope at best to wed another servant, at worst to provide an occasional diversion for the master of the house.

Jenna quickly pushed the thought away, for it was a discomforting one. But for a quirk of fate she might have been in a similar situation herself. As it was she wasn't certain her position wasn't actually worse. Even married to Gerald Fordyce—something she loathed to comtemplate— and safe from retribution, he would never cease to remind her of the debt of gratitude she owed him. His scorn would haunt her for the rest of her life. If she had been trasported, at least that suffering would end after seven years had she contrived to survive the hardship, and she would have been free.

The maid cast her a curious look. "Ambition, ma'am. I'm not sure I know what that means?"

Pushing the discomforting thoughts to the back of her mind, Jenna replied, "It is the desire to improve your situation."

The maid smiled to reveal several pretty dimples. "I just hope to go on being a lady's maid. *Your* lady's maid, ma'am."

"I don't see why not, Grace. I am very satisfied with your services."

"Mr Fordyce," the girl's cheeks coloured slightly, "says we are like to go to London for the Season."

Jenna looked away, for the matter had not been discussed with her. "Yes, that is very possible." She closed the top drawer of the commode thoughtfully. "Grace, I did wonder if you had been reorganising the drawers of the commode."

The maid was all at once concerned. "You didn't tell me to do so, ma'am."

"I know that, but I wondered if you had done it anyway."

"No, ma'am, I haven't. Is anything amiss?"

Jenna cast her a reassuring smile. "It is of no real matter, Grace, only I fancied someone had been moving my belongings."

"I always keep everything as it is, ma'am."

Jenna was still thoughtful. "Yes, I know you do."

"But I cannot speak for the other servants, ma'am. Shall I tell Mrs Tarrand?"

The thought of questioning the housekeeper on such a trifling matter was to daunting for Jenna to contemplate and she answered quickly, "I beg of you not to trouble. I am being fanciful, I fear."

The girl went on with her work, saying, "You must take care, ma'am. Someone might be looking for valuables."

Jenna laughed. "Then there is no cause to worry, for I have none."

"There's the locket, ma'am. You wouldn't want to lose that."

"I didn't know it existed until Bill Smith produced it."

The girl gave her a pitying look which was a disconcerting experience for Jenna. "Oh 'tis a real shame, ma'am, really it is. Those tinkers must be ever so wicked."

Jenna had no wish to enter into a discussion about the gypsies and asked quickly, "Have you almost finished?"

Grace gathered up a few pieces of Jenna's discarded clothing. "Yes, ma'am. I'll just take these down to the laundry. The sprigged musling is so pretty, Miss Ransome. It becomes you so well."

"When it is laundered you may have it," Jenna replied.

The maid looked astonished, as well she might be. "Miss Ransome, 'tis a new gown. I cannot. . . ."

"Mrs Fordyce ordered far too many for my needs. Please accept it."

Grace's eyes grew bright. "Oh, ma'am, how can I ever thank you?"

"By going about your duties," Jenna replied, turning away to look out of the window.

The door clicked shut. Jenna knew she had been foolish and regretted her generous impulse already, but she had felt so guilty that she had so much and Grace so little. In the sprigged muslin gown Grace was bound to look even more fetching, not that Jenna cared if Gerald found the maidservant to his taste. No, it was not Gerald who troubled her. . . .

In an effort to exorcise her uncomfortable thoughts she picked up her shawl, tossed it around her shoulders and hurried out of the room. She had ti in mind to seek out Harriet Fordyce for she was the only person with whom Jenna could converse easily, and she felt in dire need of company just then to divert her uncomfortable ruminations.

Jenna also wondered when Susannah Fairfax would call again, for it was certain she would, if only in the hope of seeing Charles Hollingdale. All Jenna's thoughts seemed to come back to him, she mused, feeling rather cross.

On rounding the corner of the corridor, however, she stopped in her tracks, for there was Grace in conversation with the object of Jenna's thoughts. He was leaning languidly against the wall, his arms folded, a half smile on his lips. Every iota of his attention was focused on the maid. It was as if she were the only woman in the world who existed for him at that moment.

Watching him exert all his considerable charm on her own maidservant was infuriating to Jenna, although she really wasn't sure why, but before she could stop herself, she snapped, "Grace! Why are you still up here? Take those garments to the laundry immediately."

The girl's face grew red and Jenna immediately regretted her harshness. However, Grace bobbed a curtsey and hurried away, whereupon Charles Hollingdale turned to Jenna, the half smile on his lips.

"Well, Miss Ransome, you have completed the transformation from gypsy to lady of the manor very quickly and exceeding well."

His smile infuriated her as much as his astuteness filled her with fear. "How dare you mock me?" she cried.

Without thinking she made to strike him, but he saw the gesture and caught her hand in his before it was able to find its mark. His smile faded as he gazed unflinchingly at her.

"You had best take heed, Cousin," he said softly, "the facade of the lady is slipping."

"You cannot expect miracles," she told him breathlessly, twisting her wrist which he kept tightly imprisoned in his grip.

"I have already witnessed one."

He pulled her inexorably closer, despite her futile struggles to free her wrist. "Charles," she begged "unhand me, I beg of you."

"At last you have spoken my name," he whispered, drawing her closer, his hand gripping her waist.

"I shall do so in future if only you will free me."

He looked down into her eyes in which he must surely recognise her fear and longing. "You don't want me to free you, Annabel," he told her, his voice harsh. "Ask me again and I will do so."

His lips touched hers tentatively at first and then with more certainty. The kiss was sweet and gentle, and although Jenna knew it was a scene he had enacted countless times in many place with innumerable women, just then she felt it was the first and only time for both of them. It was as though her life had been leading to just this moment and if it held no more joy it would have been worthwhile. They were no longer in the corridor of Barnston Manor, no longer of a mortal world. Jenna was transported into another place and she was quite certain it must be so for him too.

So engrossed were they in each other neither heard approaching footsteps until a shocked voice broke into that heavenly idyll.

"Ye Gods! What a precious sight!"

Shocked at the sound of Gerald's voice, Jenna drew away and this time Charles allowed her to go. His cousin was standing unsteadily a few yards away from them, his face red with fury. Jenna's cheeks grew red and the realisation he

125

could not mistake her own passionate response to Charles Hollingdale's practised embrace.

"I thought you would have had the decency to leave *her* alone," Gerald shouted his voice thick.

Every servant in the house must have been able to hear. The other man gazed at him implacably. It was difficult for Jenna to reconcile him with the tender lover of a few moments ago.

"Why should I?" he retorted in a quiet, yet steely voice. "You do not. And who are you to speak of decency, Fordyce? It is not a quality you have ever possessed."

Gerald's face twisted with fury as he lunged forward at his cousin. Jenna screamed and her hands flew to her lips. But Geral was foxed and no match for his cousin who easily deflected the attempted strike and hit the younger man instead.

Once again Jenna screamed, shrinking back against the panelling as Gerald fell back against the wall, hitting his head and sinking slowly to the floor in a daze.

"Foxed at this time of the day," Charles said in disgust as he towered over the sprawled figure. "You exceed your own depths of depravity, Fordyce."

"There was no need to do that!" Jenna cried, sinking down on her knees at Gerald's side.

Blood was seeping from his nose and a cut at the side of his lips. Gently she eased her arm around his shoulders and, fighting back her own tears, began to dab at the blood with her handkerchief.

A few servants followed by Harriet Fordyce came hurrying to see what had caused the fracas. Grace, on seeing Gerald lying in the corridor, gasped and began to weep. Mrs Tarrand looked stony-faced but when Jenna looked up it seemed that the look in the housekeeper's eyes was one of satisfaction.

"What has happened?" Harriet Fordyce asked, looking from Charles to Jenna. Neither answered and she said in disgust, "Brawling, I'll warrant. Over what?"

"Me," Jenna replied in a small voice. "Don't you think we should send for a physician?"

"He'll live," Charles told her and Jenna cast him a reproachful look as Mrs Fordyce sank down on her knees at her son's side. "Had I wished to put an end to him it would have been easy enough."

"How foolish you both are," Harriet Fordyce murmured and then, looking up at her nephew, "can you not see where Annabel's affections lie, Charles?"

"Let her speak for herself, Aunt."

Jenna kept her face averted, unable to speak. Mrs Fordyce took in a deep breath, "Why do you persit in distressing everyone, Charles?"

Jenna did look up at him then, her eyes full of misery. There was nothing but pain inside her, a pain which would remain with her always.

"It is clear now," he said heavily and Jenna's misery was even greater. "It is as well, in the circumstances, I have to go away for a while."

All the time he refused to look directly at Jenna who was inwardly screaming for him to stay, longing to tell him how much she loved him.

"That would be best," his aunt replied, returning her attention to her son.

He looked at Jenna at last, but she sould read nothing into his expression, not love, nor loathing. Then he turned on his heel and hurried away, and Jenna knew then that he carried her heart with him. She had known him such a short while and yet surreptitiously he had crept into her affections and she knew she would never feel the same passion for another man.

127

Gerald began to stir, moaning softly, and Jenna transferrd her attention to him once again. "Gerald," she whispered. "Oh, Gerald, I'd as lief hurt myself as have this happen to you."

"We both know it was not your fault," Mrs Fordyce whispered, and then to the wide-eyed lackeys looking on, "Help Mr Fordyce to his room."

Tears were streaming down Jenna's face as the two servants raised Gerald to his feet. Mrs Fordyce leaned forward to pat her hand. "Do not allow that scapegrace to put you out of countenace. His advances only prove he believes you to be Annabel. Now he acknowledges he can have no claim to the fortune, save through you. If we are fortunate he might never return.

The prospect made Jenna sob even harder as Mrs Fordyce said bitterly. "It is unforgivable that he should overset you in this way. He must know you and Gerald are very much attached. It is obvious to everyone who has seen you together. Let us hope we have seen the last of Major Charles Hollingdale!"

Her wish echoed in Jenna's mind, as dire as the judge's sentence upon her. If she was never to see him again, life would be unbearable indeed.

THIRTEEN

"I wonder where Hollingdale has gone?" Gerald mused one morning over breakfast.

Since his fight with his cousin he had made a conscious effort to rise early, be pleasant to Jenna and to drink a little less than before. Jenna had the feeling his mother had expressly ordered him to do so.

"Do you care?" Jenna responded and could not keep the bitterness out of her voice.

"Not overmuch, I own," he admitted, filling his mouth with food, "but it is always wise to keep one eye open when Cousin Charles is about."

"One of yours is still bruised," Jenna took pleasure in pointing out.

The young man scowled, evidently not liking the reminder. "That, as you must recall, was entirely your fault."

"Not entirely. I did not ask you to attack Major Hollingdale. There was no cause for you to do so."

"Would you have preferred me to wait until he had seduced you entirely?"

Her cheeks grew pink. "There was no possibility of that, Gerald."

He appeared unconvinced. "From where I was standing, my dear, it looked entirely possible, and recall you are my

129

future wife. I'm in no mind to be cuckolded, either before or after our marriage."

Jenna's spirits sank at the reminder of what her future was to be. If only it was Charles Hollingdale she was to marry, but she knew she must not rail too much and certainly not when Gerald could become aware of it.

"I wouldn't have thought it mattered to you," she said accusingly. "I deemed the money was your only consideration."

"Are you sorry he has gone?" Gerald asked.

His eyes challenged hers and she could not meet them. "How can you think so after what happened? I was never so mortified."

He stroked his chin thoughtfully. "As I recall you were not struggling when I happened upon you."

"As if I could. He has the strength of an ox."

"Now, now," Mrs Fordyce interrupted in a warning tone. "You must not quarrel. It is unseemly and futile now that success is in our grasp."

Gerald laughed. "Mama, you need not fret when Annabel and I quarrel, for I like her spirit. A man soon grows weary of a totally subservient wife. We shall deal very well together, much better than I ever dared hope at the outset of this affair."

"I own if you had seen Annabel's concern you would have had no cause to doubt her affection for you," Mrs Fordyce agreed.

"That might well be, but my cousin has an insidious way with women and my future wife is unused to men of his kind."

"I suppose you claim to be a paragon," Jenna could not help but retort.

Mrs Fordyce folded her copy of *The Morning Post* and put it by her plate. "Well I for one cannot help but be glad he has gone. I was for ever in a fidge when he was here and I know he alarmed Annabel."

As Jenna could not agree she remained silent. Since Charles Hollingdale's departure the house had seemed empty, like her heart. Belatedly she realised just seeing him, being in his company, was a joy. She knew even if she did not belong body and soul to Gerald Fordyce, Charles could never be hers. He was not meant for any one woman, nor a life of domesticity. It seemed perverse that it was not in her fate to love Gerald instead. How much more simple life would be if she could find it in her heart to do so.

"Except that we do not know where he has gone," Gerald pointed out.

"Does it matter as long as he has gone?" Jenna asked.

"My dear girl," he said in a tone he might adopt with the very stupid, "I am still not persuaded he will relinquish the inheritance so easily."

His mother laughed. "Oh, do not be such a bufflehead, Gerald. He has no cause to do anything else now."

The young man grunted his agreement. "There is probably some lightskirt awaiting him in London."

"Oh, I am quite persuaded he has rejoined his regiment," Harriet Fordyce contradicted.

Jenna's hand clenched convulsively on the table top. "He made no mention of it."

"He is not obliged to," Gerald told her, helping himself to another portion of eggs. "It is very like him to remain as close as oak on the matter just to make us wonder. Mayhap he is back in Spain at this very moment."

Jenna wanted to cry out in alarm so badly she was obliged to bite her lip to prevent it.

"If he does return," Harriet Fordyce mused, "which I do doubt, Annabel can always bar him from the house. After your fight, and the fact you two will be betrothed, it would be justified."

Gerald looked pleased at the idea. "What a splendid notion, Mama. 'Tis the simplest remedy."

"No," Jenna said in a quiet but resolute voice and they both turned to look at her. "It would be foolish," she went on quickly. "We must not have Major Hollingdale as an enemy."

"Annabel is perfectly correct," Mrs Fordyce agreed, looking to her son for confirmation. "At least when he is here we know exactly what he is about."

Gerald laughed scornfully. "Anyone who thinks so is a chuckle-head, Mama."

"I wish you would not credit him with an astuteness he does not possess."

"It would be an error to underestimate him," her son insisted.

"Can we not talk about something or somebody else?" Jenna pleaded. "The subject is becoming wearisome to me."

"What a splendid suggestion," Harriet Fordyce agreed. "It is much more agreeable to discuss your betrothal."

All at once Jenna was sorry she had spoken. "Is it not too soon to consider the matter?"

"I think not," Gerald replied. "When I was in Town last a crony of mine became betrothed to a chit of only two weeks' acquaintance."

"Next week we are invited to the Athertons. After that I think we should arrange our own little rout here at the Manor and use it as a time to announce the betrothal. It would be rather opportune I believe."

She looked from one to the other for agreement and her son let out a long sigh. "That sounds eminently agreeable," he replied.

Mrs Fordyce looked to Jenna then. "What do you think, my dear?"

"It is kind of you to ask, but it has nothing to do with me. Do as you believe fit."

Harriet Fordyce looked pleased, her son unconcerned.

"You are a very fortunate young woman, as I am sure you are aware. My son is more eligible than any you are like to have met, even if you had not become embroiled in those unsavoury events which overtook you a few months ago. However, I am quite persuaded you are fond of my son, which is of no surprise to me. There are few enough young women of sensibility who would not leap at the opportunity to marry him."

Her son got up and stretched to full height. "Does it matter if she finds the notion conducive or not, Mama?"

"Dealing pleasantly together is always best, despite the number of marriages of convenience which take place."

He smiled without mirth, glancing at Jenna. "Annabel will find marriage to me pleasant enough."

To Jenna his words sounded more like a threat and she shuddered. A moment later he asked, "I am going for a ride. Do you wish to accompany me, Annabel?"

She hesitated but then pushed back her chair. "Yes, of course I would. Why not?"

As they walked towards the door together he said, "I am persuaded you and I will deal well together, Annabel. In your own way you are as greedy and selfish as I am."

She paused by the door to look up at him. "How little you know me, Gerald."

He grinned in a way she was beginning to find loathsome. "Ah, but very soon, I shall know you much, much better."

It was all she could do to suppress a shudder as she preceded him out of the room.

"That was a most agreeable evening," Harriet Fordyce declared as their carriage turned into the drive of Barnston Manor.

"Frederick Atherton is a splendid host," her son agreed, his voice slightly thick.

"Because he possesses an abundance of good wine?"

133

Jenna asked, sitting back in the squabs and eyeing him coldly.

"That is a very good reason. However, you were not averse to the attentions of Mr Jonathan Atherton, so I trust the evening was successful for you too."

Jenna smiled. "His attention is not so surprising as I am a considerable heiress. You are not the only man with an avaricious nature."

He frowned. "Always remember whose fortune it really is Annabel."

"If I do not you will remind me."

"Be certain of it," he vowed.

"Mr Atherton remarked upon the way you were normally attentive towards me, so I dare say he was hoping to hear me declare our status and so know if he may pay court to me in earnest."

"What did you tell him?" Mrs Fordyce asked, pleasantly but at the same time with underlying anxiety.

"I told him I was exceeding fond of my cousin."

"That was very clever of you, my dear," he replied. "Now our betrothal will come as a surprise to no one. Everyone will know the truth of the matter before long," Gerald promised, something which made Jenna laugh although it was without mirth.

"The *truth*, Gerald?"

"The truth as we wish everyone to know it."

"An announcement will be made next week," Mrs Fordyce said thoughtfully, "and the wedding can take place in September. I believe that is eminently suitable."

The carriage drew up outside the main entrance to the Manor. As Jenna looked up it seemed that every window was ablaze with lights. The expense of the Manor's upkeep must have been enormous. Never for one moment did Jenna regard it as her home, or the fortune as hers. She had accepted the outward trappings of wealth and position as a part of the role she was to play, but she could not feel she was an heiress however hard she tried, nor would she ever be important in Gerald's life. Once the fortune was his, he would cast her aside as contemptuously as his soiled neckcloths. It was as if Jenna existed in a strange limbo, for the naive girl who trusted everyone and was companion to Aunt Zillah seemed a stranger to her now. She no longer knew who she was or what she was to do.

Gerald helped both ladies from the carriage and they walked slowly up the steps together, enjoying the freshness of the night air. Gerald negotiated the steps with a less than steady gait.

"Wherever we go," Jenna told them in a conversational tone, "I am treated like a fairytale princess awakened from a long sleep."

Mrs Fordyce chuckled. "That must be very nice for you, dear."

"It would be if it were true, but, of course, because it is not, I do feel a trifle guilty whenever people fuss over me."

"You have no cause to feel guilt," Gerald told her with a frown. "The fortune should have been mine. I was always uncle's favourite and you are only putting to rights a wrong."

"It should have been Annabel's fortune," Jenna corrected.

"But poor Annabel is dead," Mrs Fordyce pointed out. She seemed to relish the knowledge.

As they entered the hall Jenna drew a heartfelt sigh. "Yes, I know. Poor Annabel. Had she lived I wonder what she would have looked like."

"You," Gerald told her, his brows knitted into a frown once more. "An attack of conscience on your part is an unlooked-for complication for which I have no sympathy."

Jenna pushed the cloak back from her head and smiled at him. "It is certain *you* would not suffer an attack of conscience, Gerald."

135

No sooner had they set foot in the house than the library door opened and Charles Hollingdale stepped out. All three of them stiffened and Jenna's heart began to pound so loudly she feared they would all hear it.

"You're back," she gasped, gladness flooding through her, despite her innate fear of him.

"What are you doing here?" Gerald demanded, stepping forward, a ferocious look on his face. Jenna was afraid he might attack his cousin once more and be humiliated again, but it transpired Gerald was in no mood to suffer a repeat thrashing even though drink had rendered him bold.

Charles Hollingdale, by comparison, looked totally at ease, as if the altercation with Gerald had never happened. He was nursing a glass of brandy and he looked immediately at Jenna whose gladness must have been very apparent. "I have returned to my family. Do you allow me back, Annabel? It is your house we are in."

Gerald gasped with annoyance but could not gainsay him. "Yes," she replied in no more than a whisper, her eyes suddenly moist. How much better life seemed when he was there. The future did not appear quite so black.

"You must excuse our surprise," his aunt told him, recovering from her astonishment. Her tone, however, contained no warmth or welcome.

Charles Hollingdale smiled wryly, quite unperturbed by their hostility which must have been apparent. "I realised how foolish it was for me to stay away. After all I have few kin. In truth, I have no wish to live in discord with those remaining. Fordyce, I apologise for what passed between us. If you are willing, let us be friends."

Gerald Fordyce looked suspicious. After what proved to be an awkward silence he replied, "Very well." His tone echoed his reluctance. "After all it was I who attacked you and I was foxed, I own."

"But I reacted too harshly." Charles Hollingdale smiled

again. "I am vastly relieved to hear you say you forgive my impetuous behaviour."

"And so are we all relieved," his aunt told him, injecting some warmth into her voice. "Welcome back, Charles."

He inclined his head slightly. "Thank you, Aunt Harriet."

"Let us break open a bottle of champagne together," Gerald suggested.

"What a splendid idea!" the other man agreed.

Jenna, who had been unable to take her eyes away from Charles Hollingdale, at last looked away. "Pray excuse me; I am very tired."

Major Hollingdale was immediately concerned. "Does that mean you do not forgive me, Annabel!"

"It means I am tired," she reiterated.

Coldness was her only refuge. He must never know how profoundly he affected her, and most important of all, neither must Gerald and his mother.

She started up the stairs and Harriet Fordyce began to follow. "You two are welcome to crack open a bottle, but on your own. I am tired, too. No doubt you will finish the evening a trifle bosky, but it is of no account. Goodnight, gentlemen."

Jenna continued up the stairs, followed by the older woman. When she reached the top she paused and glanced back. Gerald had already gone into the library, but Charles remained in the doorway, watching her. His eyes met hers briefly, for she quickly looked away and hurried on to the sanctuary of her room where Grace was waiting, eager to hear all about the evening's events.

"Life'll be a bit more lively now Major Hollingdale is back," the girl commented as she put Jenna's gown in the press.

Jenna cast her a quick glance as she climbed into the enormous four-poster. "You like Major Hollingdale, don't you, Grace?"

137

The girl blushed. "Everyone likes Major Hollingdale, ma'am, don't they? Will you be wantin' anything else?"

Jenna shook her head. "You may retire too now, Grace. Good-night."

"Good-night, ma'am."

She backed out of the room and as soon as she had gone the silence closed in about Jenna. Closing her eyes she tried to summon sleep but her mind was filled with thoughts of Charles Hollingdale and her joy at his return. How odd it was she should have lost her heart to him. After being rescued from Newgate by Gerald Fordyce she had determined never to believe in another as long as she lived, but she had allowed her distrust to be breached and from a most unlikely quarter. Charles Hollingdale was no more trustworthy than any of the others and his apparent humility this evening was something she did not believe in for one moment.

The night was a warm one. Sleep was as far away as ever. Lying there wakeful she had heard several pairs of footsteps pass her room and she wondered if the men had yet retired. Knowing Gerald as she did now, it was certain he would not take too long to consume the champagne and would, as like or not, press his cousin to crack open another bottle.

After a while she abandoned any thought of sleep and swung her legs out of the bed, not troubling to light a candle, for she knew exactly where every piece of furniture was situated. On previous sleepless evenings, when memories had forced sleep away, she had studied the room and its contents by moonlight, conjuring up images of the elegant Marguerite moving around, sitting at the dressing-table, admiring her reflection in the cheval mirror with her jewellery sparkling in the candlelight.

This time Jenna went barefoot across the room and pulled back the curtain, allowing moonlight to flood in. She flung open one half of the casement at the same time as inhaling gladly of the still night air and its scent of honeysuckle and roses.

There were times when she thought she might never forget the stench of Newgate. The experience of being incarcerated in that wretched place had served to heighten her awareness of the good things in life; the soft perfume of a summer flower, the play of shadow and sunlight on a gravel path, the aroma of cooking, and the cry of the birds as they wheeled overhead. It was as if she had never been truly aware of them before.

Leaning out a little farther she could see that a few of the downstairs rooms were still lighted, indicating that someone was still abroad. Just as she was about to withdraw from the window Jenna became aware of a movement. At first she thought it must be the clouds edging across the moon, but then, when the shadow moved again, she realised that someone was out there. Without being aware of it her fingers clutched onto the heavy velvet curtain. A moment later she recognised who it was—Charles Hollingdale—and he was not out there alone. He was walking slowly along the path, his head inclined towards the cloaked figure which was close by his side. Suddenly they both stopped and he looked down at his companion, drawing the cloak from its head. It was then that Jenna gasped, for she recognised the fair head of her own maidservant outlined clearly in the moonlight. Jenna's eyes grew wide as she watched him cup the girl's face in his hands and kiss her tenderly.

At last she turned away, tears blurring her vision. Sobs began to rack her body as she rested her burning cheeks on the cool wall, and she wept unashamedly, as if the tears could erase all her feelings of loneliness and misery. In fact they only heightened them.

FOURTEEN

As the door shut with a loud click Jenna awoke with a start.

"Sorry I'm late, ma'am, but it couldn't be helped."

Jenna realised then that it was Mrs Tarrand who had come into her room and as the curtain remained pulled back from the previous evening sunlight flooded in.

Mrs Tarrand came across the room with a tray bearing a cup of chocolate. Jenna sat up in the bed, a dull ache hammering at her temples. "Where is Grace this morning?" she asked harshly, recalling immediately the events she had witnessed in the garden.

Mrs Tarrand put the tray down on the table and immediately went to close the window. "Grace is indisposed today, ma'am, and you will be too if you leave the window open. The air is really chill this morning."

Jenna's eyes narrowed. "Mrs Tarrand, what ails Grace?"

"A chill, I believe. It's nothing serious but I considered it best that she stay in bed today. I am sure you will agree with me, ma'am."

"Chills can become serious, Mrs Tarrand, fatally so," Jenna said with deliberate cruelty. "If she is no better tomorrow I shall insist upon sending for a physician."

Mrs Tarrand was unperturbed. "As you wish, ma'am, but I expect you'll find her recovered by then."

Jenna realised then that the housekeeper had the sprigged muslin gown over her arm. "What are you doing with that?"

The woman smiled grimly. "I've brought it up from the laundry, ma'am. I thought you might wish to wear it this morning."

"I gave it to Grace. Did she not tell you?"

"Yes, she did, but I'm afraid I cannot allow her to accept it."

Jenna found herself growing angry. "I insist that she does, Mrs Tarrand."

Again the housekeeper smiled grimly. "It would set a bad example for the others."

The woman went to hang it in the press and Jenna argued no longer, for it was not, after all, her loss. Suddenly Jenna realised there was something else odd about Mrs Tarrand this morning. There was an air of suppressed excitement about her and oddly her eyes were red-rimmed as if she too had spent a good deal of the night weeping.

Coming back to the bed the woman said, "Ruby'll be along with the water and to help you dress. I'm sure you will find her satisfactory in Grace's absence."

"No doubt, but it won't be necessary to take Ruby away from her other duties. I contrived for long enough without a maid, but I would like some breakfast on a tray up here. Bread and butter will do. I am not very hungry this morning."

"Very well, ma'am. I shall see it's attended to immediately. Will there be anything else?"

Jenna shook her head and when the housekeeper had gone she got out of bed. She went straight to the window to look out, as if the lovers might still be there. The garden

141

was both deserted and still. When, a few minutes later, Ruby arrived with the hot water Jenna instructed her to put out her riding habit, for she was very anxious to be out of the house. The more she was away from it, the less she was likely to encounter Charles Hollingdale.

The river rippled ever so slightly in the breeze. Jenna stared down into its murky depths as she sat with her back against the broad trunk of an oak. She had lost track of how long she had been there, but her horse, tethered to a low branch, snickered restlessly. Her riding-hat, whip and gloves lay on the turf at her side while she systematically and absent-mindedly stripped a fallen branch of its leaves.

Suddenly, in the distance, she heard the pounding of hooves. She stiffened and then looked around in alarm, half expecting to see Gerald come in search of her, but she shrank back against the tree-trunk when she realised it was Charles and not his cousin. He slowed the horse as he approached and then when he was a few yards away he dismounted, tethering his horse alongside her own.

Jenna did not acknowledge his presence even when his shadow fell across her lap.

"I was concerned for you when you didn't appear for breakfast this morning."

"I wasn't hungry."

He sat down at her side on the turf. "I've been looking for you all over the estate."

"I'm sorry you've been put to so much trouble."

"It's no trouble, but why have you no groom with you?"

"I wished to be alone. I'm not accustomed to being accompanied wherever I ride."

"I did want to talk to you." She looked at him in alarm and he smiled faintly. "Gerald will not interrupt us on this occasion. He is still sleeping off his stupor. I'm afraid I

142

allowed him the larger share of the bottle we cracked open last night."

She couldln't help but smile. "You are indeed devious."

"He did not need to be coaxed, I assure you."

"I am certain he did not."

He looked suddenly serious. "Do you mind if I stay and talk?"

Jenna looked away from him, for she was very much tempted to laugh. If only he knew how much she wanted him to stay, that she only felt alive in his presence even knowing him for a treacherous and unprincipled rake.

"You may stay if you wish."

"Do *you* wish?"

After a moment she drew in a sharp breath. "Yes," and then, "We thought you had gone back to your regiment."

"I am seriously considering resigning my commission." She cast him a curious look and he added, "I have other plans for the future." After a moment he sent a pebble hurtling into the water. "You still haven't forgiven me."

"You are quite mistaken. Gentlemen fight for no real reason all the while. It is of no account to me."

"I wasn't thinking of the fight." There was another pause and then he said, making her start, "It was only a kiss."

"No doubt but I am not used to being fickle although I doubt there will be any lasting harm."

He leaned a little closer. "What I wished to say was, it was only a kiss but sufficient to prove we belong together." Her head jerked back and she stared at him wide-eyed. His hand reached out for her. "Let us not mince words. Ever since the day I arrived when we bumped into one another we have both known an undeniable truth—we belong together."

Her heart began to beat unevenly and the unbearable part was his look of utter sincerity. "That is absurd," she protested, jerking her hand away from his.

"I think you know it is not."

"And I am persuaded your words have been spoken more often than any written by Mr Sheridan, and to as diverse an audience."

He chuckled softly and laid his head back on the tree-trunk. "Oh my love, I cannot deny my past ways—I will not call them wrongs. There have been many women in my life, some of whom I even believed I loved, but it is nothing to how I feel for you."

There was a lump in her throat which refused to budge. How she longed to believe him or even to pretend that she did. Even more difficult was suppressing her own declaration of love.

Instead she said with cold deliberation, "I suppose the Ransome inheritance has little to do with it."

His eyes narrowed. "I have no designs on a fortune. I have sufficient of my own."

She smiled bitterly. "How gallant you are. Well, even if you are sincere . . ."

He frowned. "Do you doubt it? Can you not see quite clearly that I am speaking the truth from the depths of my heart?"

Jenna felt as if she were being rent apart. In a voice choked with emotion she told him, "You should know, Charles, I am betrothed to Gerald."

Her words were received in silence and she dare not look at him. At length he said in a harsh whisper, "So soon? I cannot credit that."

"We have known each other sufficient time. The announcement is to be made next week."

"It need not. Mistakes in such matters are commonplace. No announcement has been made and you may change your mind."

"I shall not."

Still she dare not look at him. At last he said, "I know my cousin can use a smooth tongue when he wishes. I have seen him fill foolish chits with flummery, but you are not of that ilk."

"I am gratified to hear you say so."

His voice grew angry as he said, "I cannot conceive that you love him. Admit that you do not!"

She laughed and her laughter had an edge of hysteria about it. "Can you not imagine anyone resisting your honeyed tongue in favour of another, Charles?"

His anger faded as quickly as it had come. "This is not a matter of *pride*. 'Tis our future happiness." When she made no reply he asked, "If you had not already accepted Fordyce would you have agreed to marry me?"

The question was too painful for her to answer. Instead she closed her eyes and laid her head back against the tree. However he was not to be denied an answer. He reached out and turned her face towards his. Her eyes brimmed with tears as yet unshed. Moments later he let her go, getting quickly to his feet. He brushed off his breeches with an impatient hand.

"This matter is not yet resolved whatever you may say to the contrary."

"For me it is. There is nothing more to say."

"We shall see," he vowed and then in a softer voice, "Trust me. I shall prove to you it is not a fortune I am seeking, just your love and companionship for the rest of our days."

Jenna closed her eyes in a futile attempt to blot out her anguish. She neither answered nor looked at him and a few moments later she heard him ride away. As the hoofbeats faded into the distance she buried her head in her lap and once again indulged in the luxury of tears.

"My dear, you look a trifle hollow-eyed this evening," Harriet Fordyce observed as they sat over dinner that evening.

Jenna had eaten little and spoken even less. She had been tempted not to come down at all, but knew she could not spend the rest of her life running away from Charles Hollingdale, however painful his presence might be.

"I trust you are not sickening for a chill," Gerald added, looking at her curiously. "You were out riding an unconscionably long time this morning."

"Perhaps. I do have a slight chill. I don't know."

Charles, with whom she had exchanged few words since arriving back at the house, cracked a nut and observed, "We must all remember what a transition she has been obliged to make. Such strains are bound to show after a while."

"Indeed," his aunt agreed. "We have been a trifle thoughtless, I fear, and we shall have to ensure we do not attend too many social occasions in the next few weeks. Meetings so many new people, not to mention family and adjusting to an entirely new way of life, is bound to have affected her."

Jenna was glad enough to allow them to make excuses for her and she pushed back her chair. "If you will excuse me now I would like to retire early tonight. I didn't sleep too well last night."

Charles Hollingdale sat back in the chair and eyed her almost insolently. "Why do you not confess you still have the gypsy spirit and miss sleeping under the stars?"

Two tiny spots of colour tinged her otherwise pale cheeks. "I cannot say why I was so wakeful. I . . . thought I heard noises in the garden at one point. Mayhap that is what kept me from sleep."

"What manner of noises?" Charles asked, looking disinterested.

"I thought someone was out there."

"It was possibly some of the servants taking the air before retiring," Mrs Fordyce suggested.

"It was I," Charles admitted, "taking the air after too much champagne." Jenna was about to go past him when he caught her hand in his. "Don't go just yet, my dear. I would have you join us in the drawing-room. There is something I wish to discuss with all of you."

She stiffened as Mrs Fordyce asked, "Can it not wait until tomorrow, Charles? Annabel looks truly hag-ridden tonight."

"No, Aunt, it cannot wait. Fordyce, shall we take our port in the drawing-room this evening?"

"If you insist."

"I do." He looked up at Jenna. "Do you feel well enough to join us?"

"I am not ill," she answered dully.

"Splendid."

He too got to his feet and, throwing his napkin onto the table, Gerald did likewise. Mrs Fordyce's concern was very apparent. They were all curious.

"What do you wish to discuss so urgently?" Harriet Fordyce asked when they reached the drawing-room.

Jenna sat down in an armchair whilst Gerald went to pour two glasses of port, one of which he handed to the other man before seating himself next to his mother on the sofa. Charles Hollingdale stood in front of the fireplace, the only one of them at all at ease, the glass of port in his hand.

"Well, Hollingdale? You didn't answer Mama's question," Gerald told him. "What is it you are in such a fidge to discuss with us?"

His cousin took a sip of the port. "The Ransome

inheritance," he answered at last, reaching for the bell pull and giving it three hard tugs. At the same time he put down the glass of port on the mantel.

The other three present stiffened and Charles remained the only one at ease in the room.

"It is settled, so what is there to discuss?" Gerald asked in a belligerent tone.

"A great deal, Cousin." Charles looked at Jenna. "First of all, my dear, would you be so kind as to tell us who you really are?"

Jenna gasped and sat forward in the chair, gripping the arms. Mrs Fordyce jumped to her feet. "Charles, this is absurd. Are you foxed?"

"You know I am not, Aunt."

Her manner became less heated and she told him truculently, "You know very well who she is."

"She is not my cousin Annabel."

"Hell's teeth!" Gerald snarled. "Your attic's to let, Hollingdale."

"I am perfectly sober and my mind is not unhinged," Charles replied, and no one could doubt him. "This is not Annabel Ransome, a fact of which I have been fully aware for some time."

Gerald's face grew dark with anger. "Just what trickery are you up to, Hollingdale?"

There was no mockery in Charles Hollingdale's manner for once; he was deadly serious. "I am not about any trickery, Fordyce, although I'll wager someone else is." Again he looked at Jenna and asked, "What is your name?"

"Annabel Ransome," she answered through stiff lips. Fear pervaded every fibre of her being. He knew she was an imposter although how it had come about she could not imagine, but there was no doubt he was quite certain of the fact.

"Whoever you are, you are not Annabel Ransome and I can prove it is so."

"Stuff and nonsense," Mrs Fordyce protested, laughing uneasily. "We too had our misgivings at first but after Mr Pritchett became convinced of her authenticity we had no reason to doubt her true identity either."

"I own it has been a skilful portrayal. This young lady has been tutored well for her role, but, as I said, I knew categorically some time ago that this was not my cousin."

"How could you possibly *know*?" his aunt asked, looking at him scornfully.

"He is merely a bad loser," Gerald accused.

"Do we not both lose?" Charles asked silkily. "But perhaps not."

"What are you suggesting?" his cousin demanded.

"I am merely pointing out the truth, Cousin. Let me explain something and you will understand the better. My cousin Annabel had a large birthmark just behind her left ear. When I ascertained that this otherwise perfect creature did not, the truth was obvious."

Jenna, afraid and silent in her chair, recalled his touch when he had helped her with her cloak the night they attended the Fairfax's rout. He had indeed known for a long while. She could scarce bear to recall that all the while she had posed as Annabel Ransome he had known her for a fraud.

His aunt laughed. "Is that all? 'Tis no evidence at all. 'Tis nothing!"

Charles Hollingdale fixed her with a steely look. "I also know just where and who my real cousin happens to be."

The smile left Mrs Fordyce's face immediately. "This is preposterous. She had on her Marguerite's locket. How do you think she might have come by that if she is not Annabel Ransome?"

"I recall very well Uncle Jack giving Mama some small piece of Aunt Marguerite's jewellery after she died." His gaze lingered knowingly upon his aunt. "It is entirely possible he also gave pieces to others."

Mrs Fordyce looked outraged but she had no opportunity to protest at his apparent slur, for there came a knock on the door and Mrs Tarrand put her head timidly around the crack.

Mrs Fordyce gave a gasp of exasperation. "Mrs Tarrand, we do not wish to be disturbed. Pray go away."

"Come along in," Charles Hollingdale invited and then, glancing at his aunt, "Mrs Tarrand is here at my invitation."

Not only did the housekeeper enter the room but her niece also. Both looked unusually afraid. Grace was wearing a gown of pink chintz and her lovely fair hair was for once uncovered. She looked quite different to when Jenna normally saw her in her kerseymere gown and cap.

"Please be seated, Mrs Tarrand," Charles invited and the woman did so as he beckoned the girl towards him. He glanced at the others before he said, "Allow me to introduce Miss Grace Needham formerly Annabel Ransome."

The Fordyces looked incredulous. Jenna just stared, incapable of saying or doing anything. She merely sat up straight, feeling as if she were watching the action of a play. It was certainly nothing of which she felt a part.

"What nonsense is this?" Gerald declared, gulping back the last of his port. He half rose from the seat, putting down his empty glass. "I shall not remain in this room and see my cousin's name insulted."

"Sit down, Fordyce," his cousin ordered and so authoritative was the voice Gerald did so.

Mrs Tarrand began to weep quietly into her handkerchief whereupon Mrs Fordyce cast her an angry look. "If you expect us to believe this Banbury Tale you have more hair than wit."

"I suppose this chit bears the mythical birthmark no one else has heard about," Gerald scoffed, having recovered from the initial surprise.

"She does, but there is other proof."

The girl herself stood near Charles, clasping her hands together and staring at the Turkey carpet at her feet. Now and again she cast him a worried look. Never once did she glance at Jenna.

"Why do you think this is Annabel?" Mrs Fordyce demanded of her nephew.

"I knew Marguerite Ransome when she was first wed. This girl is almost a perfect reincarnation of her. I saw it when I first arrived and naturally she intrigued me. I questioned this girl on her origins whenever I was able, having made certain in my own mind that the heiress already here was an imposter. After my unfortunate altercation with Fordyce, I took the opportunity of travelling to Horsham where Annabel had lived most of her life. I asked questions and checked the Parish records. A Grace Needham had been born in 1790, the year after Annabel Ransome, but Grace Needham had died and was buried in the churchyard of Horsham Parish Church in 1792 aged two and a half years. This young lady appeared in the Needham household some time later and Mrs Needham explained it was her brother's child, the name being a family one. Tarry will tell you that there never was any brother.

"When I returned to the Manor yesterday I charged Tarry with what I knew."

"And needless to say she agreed this sevant girl was the missing heiress," Gerald scoffed.

"I think you should explain this, Mrs Tarrand," Harriet Fordyce told her, looking pale and, for once, unsure of herself. "My nephew is quite a tongue-pad so let us hear your account."

The housekeeper sniffed into her handkerchief. "Mr Ransome didn't care about the child. Always in London, he was, and when he was here he didn't want to see her. Too like her mother, she was, too painful, he said. I found her wandering that day, no one caring whether she lived or died. He didn't deserve a child. Aggie's little one had died of the pox and there was my poor sister fretting her life away. Annabel was near the river when I saw her, almost in, she was. I ran down to pull her out before the river could sweep her away. She was frightened and began to cry, putting her arms around my neck. That's when I decided to take her away. I picked her up and took her to my sister who brought her up to be a good and decent girl." She looked at them all accusingly through tear-washed eyes. "What would have become of her here?"

"Only recall what became of my brother!" Harriet Fordyce cried and the housekeeper looked away.

"I didn't know he'd take it to heart. I thought he'd be glad to be rid of her. With him being in London so much I thought the master would marry again to some fine London lady and fill the nursery. *They* wouldn't miss poor little Annabel, and she saved my sister's life, she did."

All of them listened in silence until Mrs Tarrand began to cry again. The girl moved then, crossing the room and kneeling by the housekeeper. "Aunt Mary, please don't cry. I've been happy. I couldn't have been happier. You've nothing to be sorry about."

"Why on earth did you bring her back?" Harriet Fordyce cried, looking around in bewilderment.

Mrs Tarrand sniffed loudly. "My sister passed on and Grace was left on her own. Then, when the master took ill, I thought . . . somehow . . . I might tell him, but I never found the courage although I did manage to put it into his mind that Annabel was alive. That's when he changed his will." Gerald groaned loudly. "I wanted to tell him but no one thought he'd get notice to quit so soon. Then, after poor Mr Ransome passed on, *she* came, posing as Miss Annabel. I can't tell you how I felt seeing her here as mistress and my little Grace working as a housemaid—the rightful heiress— and not being able to do a thing about it." She shot a hate-filled look at Jenna who sat transfixed in her chair. "At least I couldn't until Major Hollingdale faced me with it. Now I don't care what happens to me as long as Grace gets what is due to her."

"Nothing will happen to you, Aunt," the girl promised. "Major Hollingdale has vowed to me it will not."

"All this is a very likely tale," Gerald scoffed. "No doubt it was contrived between you, Hollingdale, like this birthmark which no one else knows about. It may well be a figment of your fancy."

His cousin looked grim. "It is always possible. I would not expect you to take my word for it. However, Tarry has in her possession the clothing worn by the child the day she disappeared, the description of which is well-documented. Moreover, they are embroidered with her initials."

Jenna's immediate reaction was one of relief, to be free of subterfuge and the prospect of a lifetime of pretence.

Harriet Fordyce's hand crept to her throat as if invisible fingers were squeezing it. Once again Gerald jumped to his feet, this time to point an accusing finger at Jenna.

"You're the imposter! You and that rascally gypsy contrived this, I'll be bound."

She stared back at him uncomprehendingly and then she understood. They would, of course, disown her entirely to save themselves from implication. There was nothing or no one who could connect them with her. In her fear she looked to the man she loved and he cast her a regretful look. He would not or could not help her. She was totally on her own.

153

"Gerald is correct," his mother cried. "This is an abominable hoax and someone will pay dearly for it. Who are you girl? Who sent you here? Tell us before we fetch the parish constable."

"Mrs Fordyce, please!"

The woman's face was implacable. She would show her no mercy now she had failed, even though it was through no fault of her own. Shaking her head Jenna rushed past Charles Hollingdale and out of the room.

"No!" someone cried. "Don't go. Stop! Stop!"

Even as she ran Jenna knew there was nowhere for her to go. At the realisation she threw herself against the wall and sobbed heartbrokenly.

"Don't run away."

It was Charles who was pursuing her. When he reached her she turned her damp cheeks to the wall and said in a voice heavy with misery, "You have no notion of what you have done."

"I'm sorry I was obliged to humiliate you, but you must see I could not stand by without putting the matter to rights."

"I never wanted to be Annabel Ransome," she gasped. "I'm glad the pretence is over, but . . ."

He reached out and drew her towards him. "Who are you? What is your name?"

"Jenna . . . Jenna Tregail," she answered keeping her head averted.

He smiled then, looking down into her eyes. "Jenna Tregail I love you, even without the Ransome inheritance. Now do you believe I do not want a fortune for a wife?"

Uneven laughter erupted from her at his words, words which, a short time ago would have cast her into a delight. "You love me," she gasped, "and yet you have consigned me to *hell*."

His eyes narrowed. "I know a little about that, but I don't believe we speak of the same place."

There seemed no point in hiding the matter any longer. She began in halting words to tell him about how the Fordyces had found her in Newgate Prison.

"Newgate?" he exclaimed, the moment the place was mentioned. "Hell's teeth, how did you come to arrive there? You are no felon."

"I have been a party to a fraud."

"Only by intimidation, I'll be bound."

Painful as it was she explained, sparing herself nothing. Mrs Creevy, Mr Quint, and the whole sorry story.

He drew in a sharp breath and then held her close. "My poor love," he murmured, stroking her hair. "You have been so ill-used. You have known hell indeed, but all that is at an end now. The only place to which you will go is Mile End, which is where I live. I know you love me and with me you'll be safe at last."

She broke away to look at him. "Oh, I do love you, but your cousin will certainly betray me to the law now."

"If he does he will only betray himself. Just now there is no proof he is implicated in anything other than being gullible. If you accuse him of being a part of the fraud he will deny it, and he is already ingratiating himself with my real cousin. He has a good deal to lose by betraying you."

Her demeanour immediately brightened. "That is wonderful! Even now I hardly dare believe it is true. It would be bad enough to be consigned to that place if I were a true felon, but to be inoccently imprisoned. . . . Mr Quint was the true criminal."

"You must try to put it out of your head, Jenna, or at least consign it as far back in your mind as you are able, for as I am fully aware, it is impossible to truly forget suffering."

"Yes, you know of it too," she murmured, and then,

"That poor girl. She is already half in love with Gerald, I fear."

He looked wry then. "Have no doubt Tarry will look out for her interests just as she always has done."

Jenna looked up at him. "Oh, Charles, am I truly free?"

"Not for very long, I'm afraid, only until a wedding can be arranged."

Her eyes shone with love through her tears as he kissed her gently. Her arms went about his neck to respond gladly at last. His kisses were as sweet as on the previous occasion, but this time there were no reservations for either of them.

When she drew away at last she said, "It will be devilishly awkward living here from now on."

He slipped one hand about her waist. "I have no intention of allowing you to remain a day longer. I'm going now to order a carriage to take us both to my sister who will welcome you warmly. I have already spoken to her about you."

"You haven't told her I was masquerading as Annabel, have you?"

"No. I merely told her that I had met the woman I wanted to make my wife."

Jenna relaxed against him. "I had no notion you had a sister."

He looked down at her again. "There is a good deal we have to learn about one another, my love. It is a lifetime's work, I feel."

She laid her head on his shoulder and said contentedly as he led her towards the hall, "I cannot wait to begin."